Sub Terra

Sub Terra
Mining Scenes

Baldomero Lillo

Sub-Terra. Mining Scenes

© 2019 by Daniel Bernardo

SOJOURNER BOOKS

https://sojournerbooks.com

Translated by Daniel Bernardo from

Sub Terra. Cuadros Mineros

ISBN: 978-1-989586-04-4

Table of Contents

Preface

Sub Terra. Cuadros Mineros is the first work by the Chilean short-story writer Baldomero Lillo (1867-1923), published on July 12, 1904. In its first edition it was composed of eight stories, almost all of them set in the coal mines of Lota in the Province of Concepción. In the second edition, from 1917, other five stories were added, some of them with a different theme.

The book describes from various angles and characters the way coal miners lived and died –particularly those in the Lota mines in southern Chile- in the late nineteenth and early twentieth centuries, who worked from dawn to dusk in miserable conditions.

It is basically a description of life in the mine, and the life of its workers; it is also a critique of the exploiting power, which reduced the human condition of the miners to simple beasts. Lillo was considered the master of the genre of social realism in his country.

The first edition consisted of eight stories:

> The Invalids
> Gate Number 12
> Firedamp
> Payday
> The Devil's Pit
> The Well
> Juan Fariña
> Big Game Hunting

Later, in the second edition, Lillo modified the text of several of the original stories and added:

The Search
The Drill
It was Him Alone...
The Attached Hand
Cañuela and Petaca

The Invalids

The extraction of a horse from the mine, a rare event, had grouped around the entrance to the mine the workers who dumped the wheelbarrows in the field and those in charge of returning the empty ones and placing them in the cages.

They were all old, useless for the work inside the mine, and that horse, that after ten years of dragging down the ore trains was returned to the clarity of the sun, inspired the deep sympathy that is experienced by an old and loyal friend with whom they have shared the fatigue of a hard day.

To many that beast brought back the memory of better days, when in the narrow quarry with their then vigorous arms, they plunged with a single blow into the hidden seam the steel tooth of the hewer's pickaxe. Everyone knew Diamond, the generous brute, who docile and indefatigable trotted with his train of wagons, from morning until night, in the sinuous hauling galleries. And when the overwhelming fatigue of that superhuman task paralyzed the impulse of their arms, the sight of the horse passing by, with white foam at his mouth, gave them new encouragement to continue their task of perforating ants with the unshakable tenacity of the wave that crumbles grain by grain the immovable rock that defies its rages.

All were silent at the appearance of the horse, disabled by incurable lameness for any work inside or outside the mine, and whose last stage would be the barren plain where they only perceived, in short stretches, scrub covered with dust, without a blade of grass, nor a tree interrupting the uniform and monotonous gray of the landscape.

Nothing more grim than that desolate plain, dry and dusty, sown with small mounds of sand so thick and heavy that the winds hardly carried it through the bare soil, eager for humidity.

In a small elevation of the ground, the hoist, the chimneys and the smoked sheds of the mine were raised. The miners' hamlet was situated on the right, in a small hollow. Above it a dense mass of black smoke floated heavily in the rarefied air, making the appearance of that inhospitable spot darker.

A stifling heat came out of the scorched earth, and the subtle and impalpable coal dust adhered to the sweaty faces of the workers who, leaning on their wheelbarrows savored in silence the brief rest that this maneuver gave them.

After the prescribed blows, the large pulleys at the top of the hoist began to turn slowly, sliding through their slots the thin metal threads that were coiling in the great drum, gigantic reel, the powerful machine. A few moments passed and suddenly a dark mass dripping with water rose quickly from the black pit and stopped a few meters above the rim.

Suspended in a net of thick ropes held under the cage he swung over the abyss with his legs open and stiff, a black horse. Seen from below in that grotesque posture, it resembled a monstrous spider gathered in the center of his web. After swinging for a moment in the air, it descended gently to the level of the platform. The workers rushed over that kind of sack, diverting it from the opening of the entrance of the mine, and Diamond, free in a moment of his ligatures, rose trembling on his legs and remained motionless, snorting wearily.

Like all horse mine workers, he was a small animal. The skin that was once soft, glossy and black like the jet, had lost its luster, riddled with untold scars. Large cracks and oozing wounds indicated the site of the draught harnesses, and the hock flaunted old spavins that deformed the fine legs of another time. Potbellied, with a long neck and bony haunches, he showed no remnants of the past gallantry and slenderness, and the manes of the tail had almost disappeared, torn off by the whip whose bloody imprint still looked fresh on the sunken back.

The workers looked at him with painful surprise. What a change had taken place in the spirited brute they had known! That was only a piece of nauseating meat, good for vultures and buzzards. And while the horse, blinded by the noonday light, kept his head low and motionless, the oldest of the miners, straightening his angular body, glanced around him. In his withered face, but with firm and correct lines, there was an expression of dreamy gravity and his eyes, where life seemed to have taken refuge, came and went from the horse to the silent group of his comrades, living ruins, like useless machines, that the mine threw from time to time, from its deepest depths.

The old men looked with curiosity at their companion waiting for one of those strange and incomprehensible speeches that sometimes flowed from the lips of the miner whom they considered to have a great intellectual culture, because there was always in the pockets of his blouse some unbound and dirty book whose reading absorbed his hours of rest and from which he took those phrases and terms unintelligible to his listeners.

His ordinary, resigned and sweet countenance was transfigured as he commented on the tortures and ignominies of the poor, and his word then acquired the intonation of the inspired and of the apostle.

The old man remained for an instant in a reflective attitude and then, passing his arm around the neck of the invalid nag, with a deep and vibrant voice as if haranguing a crowd exclaimed:

–Poor old horse, you are thrown out because you are no longer useful! It's the same for all of us. Down there no distinction is made between man and beasts. When our strength is exhausted, the mine throws us as the spider throws out of its web the bloodless body of the fly that served it as food. Comrades, this brute is the image of our life! Like him we remain silent, suffering our destiny resigned! And yet our strength and power are so immense that nothing under the sun would resist its thrust. If all the oppressed with their hands tied behind their backs marched against our oppressors, how quickly would we break the pride of those who today drink our blood and suck to the marrow our bones. We would throw them, in the first onslaught, like a handful of straw that disperses the hurricane. They are so few, their host is so petty before the innumerable army of our brothers that populate the workshops, the countryside and the bowels of the earth!

As he spoke, the miner's broken face cheered, his eyes hurled flames, and his body trembled in the grip of intense excitement. With his head thrown back and his gaze lost in the void, he seemed to see there in the distance the gigantic human wave, advancing through the fields with the inattentive race of the sea that had crossed its secular barriers. As under the ocean that drags the grain of sand and demolishes the mountains, everything would collapse under the formidable shock of those famished legions that waving the rag as a flag of extermination would reduce to ashes the palaces and temples, those dwellings where selfishness and arrogance have dictated the iniquitous laws that have made of the immense majority of men beings similar to beasts: Sisyphus condemned to an eternal task, the miserable ones struggle and agitate without a spark of intellectual light scratching the darkness of their slave brains where the idea, that seed, divine, will never germinate.

The workers fixed in the old man their restless pupils, where the fearful distrust of the beast that ventures in an unknown path shone. For those dead souls, each new idea was a blasphemy against the creed of servitude bequeathed to them by their grandparents, and in that comrade whose words enthused the young people of the mine, they saw only a restless and reckless spirit, an unbalanced one who dared to rebel against the immutable laws of destiny.

And when the silhouette of the foreman stood out, coming towards them, at the end of the court, each one hastened to push his wheelbarrow mixing the crunch of their dry joints when stretching the tired limbs with the squeaking of the wheels sliding on the rails.

The old man, his eyes wet and bright, saw that wretched flock move away, and then, taking the horse's stark head in his hands, caressed his meager manes, muttering in a half voice:

–Goodbye friend, you have nothing to envy us. Like you we walked burdened by a load that a slight jolt would make slide off our shoulders, but that we obstinately held until death.

And stooping over his wheelbarrow, he slowly walked away, economizing his strength as a fighter defeated by work and old age.

The horse remained in the same place, motionless, without changing its posture. The rhythmic and languid swaying of his ears and the movement of his eyelids were the only signs of life of that body full of foul scourges and protuberances. Dazzled and blinded by the vivid clarity that the transparency of the air made more radiant and intense, he bent his head, looking between his front legs for a refuge against the luminous arrows that wounded his pupils used to the darkness, unable to withstand any light other than the weak and exhausted light of the security lamps.

But that glow was everywhere and victoriously penetrated through his drooping eyelids, blinding him more and more; stunned, he took a few steps forward, and his head crashed into the board fence that limited the platform. He seemed surprised at the obstacle and, straightening his ears, he sniffed the wall, giving a brief snort of restlessness; he went back in search of a way out, coming and going, finding new obstacles between the wooden piles, the wagons, and the beams of the hoist, like a blind man who has lost his guide. As he walked, he lifted his hoofs, folding the shanks as if he were still walking among the sleepers of the track of a dragging tunnel; and a swarm of flies that buzzed around him without worrying about the abrupt contractions of the skin and the feverish turning of the naked tail, harassed him fiercely, multiplying his ferocious attacks.

By his beast's brain had to come across the vague idea that he was in a corner of the mine which he did not yet know and where an impenetrable red veil concealed the objects that were familiar to him.

His stay there ended very soon: a stableman came with a roll of ropes under his arm and going straight towards him, tied him by his neck and, pulling the halter, he went, followed by the horse, along the road whose black ribbon was going to be lost in the scorched plain that stretched everywhere its arid surface towards the limit of the horizon.

Diamond limped atrociously and from his old dark skin ran a painful shudder produced by the contact of the rays of the sun, which from the blue sided of the skies seemed pleased to light that rag of throbbing flesh so that the voracious vultures, almost imperceptible points lost in the void, could stalk their prey, which his good luck had given them.

The driver stopped at the edge of a depression in the terrain. He untwisted the knot that oppressed the flaccid neck of the prisoner, clapped his hands hard on the rump to force him to go on forward; then he turned around and went back the same way he had come.

That hollow was covered by a layer of water in the rainy season, but the heat of the summer quickly evaporated it. In the lower parts there was some moisture where small thorny shrubs grew and one or the other bunch of dry and dusty grass. In hidden places there were tiny pools of muddy water, but they were inaccessible to any animal no matter how agile and vigorous it was.

Diamond, plagued by hunger and thirst, walked a short distance, inhaling the air noisily. From time to time he would put his lips in contact with the sand and snort loudly, lifting clouds of whitish powder through the lower layers of the air that seemed to be boiling above that fire floor.

His blindness did not diminish and his pupils contracted under his eyelids only perceiving that intense red flame that had replaced in his brain the now distant vision of the shadows of the mine.

Suddenly a penetrating buzz ripped the air, followed immediately by a whinny of pain, and the miserable nag began to jump and run with the speed that his deformed legs and weak forces allowed him, through the bushes and depressions of the terrain. Above him fluttered a dozen great sand horseflies.

Those fierce enemies gave him no truce, and very soon he stumbled into a wide crack, and his body became as if embedded in the cleft. He made some useless efforts to get up, and convinced of his helplessness stretched his neck and resigned himself with the passivity of the brute to death putting an end to the pains of his tormented flesh.

The horseflies, fed up with blood, ceased their attacks, their wings and armored bodies flashing as if they were precious stones, pierced the warm air and disappeared like golden arrows in the splendid blue of the sky, whose clear transparency did not tarnish the faintest shred of the mist.

Some shadows, slipping flush with the ground, began to draw concentric circles around the fallen one. Up there, about twenty large black birds hovered in the air, the heavy fluttering of the buzzards and the majestic carriage of the vultures which, with their wings open and motionless, described immense spirals that were slowly narrowing around the limp body of the horse.

Dark spots appeared all over the horizon: they were stragglers who came beating his wings to the feast that awaited them.

In the meantime, the sun was rapidly setting. The grey of the plain took on more opaque and somber dyes at every moment. In the mine the chores had ceased and the miners like the slaves of the ergastulum left their gloomy holes. Down there they piled up in the elevator forming a compact mass, a knot of heads, legs, and intertwined arms that, out of the entrance of the mine, would laboriously unravel, becoming a long column that walked silently along the road in the direction of the distant rooms.

The old wagon-driver, sitting in his wagon, watched from the court the parade of workers whose bent torsos still seemed to feel the crushing touch of the rock in the very low galleries. Suddenly he rose and as the retreat ring of the signal bell slipped clear and vibrant in the serene atmosphere of the deserted countryside, the old man, heavy and slow to walk, went to swell the ranks of those galleons whose lives are of less value to their exploiters than a single piece of that mineral which, like a black river, flows inexhaustibly from the heart of the lode.

In the mine everything was peace and silence, there was no rumor other than the dull and rhythmic steps of the workers who were leaving. The darkness grew, and up there in the immense dome sprouted thousands of stars whose whites, opaline and purple shines, shone with increasing intensity in the twilight that enveloped the earth, already submerged in the precursory shadows of the darkness of the night.

Gate Number 12

Pablo instinctively clung to his father's legs. His ears were ringing, and the floor beneath his feet gave him a strange sense of anguish. He thought he was rushing into that hole whose black opening he had glimpsed as he entered the cage, and his big eyes were staring at the gloomy walls of the pit into which they were sinking with dizzying speed. In that silent descent without trepidation or more noise than the dripping water on the iron roof, the lights of the lamps seemed ready to be extinguished, and their faint flashes were vaguely delineated in the gloom of the indentations and protruding parts of the rock; an endless series of black shadows that flew like arrows towards the top.

After a minute the speed slowed sharply, his feet settled more solidly on the fugitive floor, and the heavy iron frame, with a rough grinding of hinges and chains, stood motionless at the entrance to the gallery.

The old man took the little one by the hand and together they went into the black tunnel. They were among the first to arrive, since the movement of the mine had not yet begun. From the gallery, high enough to allow the miner to raise his body completely, only part of the roof was distinguished, crossed by thick beams. The side walls remained invisible in the deep darkness that filled the vast and gloomy excavation.

Forty metres from the peak they stopped in front of a kind of cave excavated in the rock. From the soot-colored, cracked ceiling hung a tinleaf lamp whose muted glow gave the room the appearance of a mournful crypt full of shadows. In the background, sitting in front of a table, a small man, now aged, made notes in a huge register. His black suit highlighted the pallor of his face furrowed by deep wrinkles. At the sound of footsteps he raised his head and fixed an interrogating look on the old miner, who advanced shyly, saying in a voice full of submission and respect:

–Sir, here I bring the boy.

The foreman's piercing eyes glanced over the boy's flimsy body. His thin limbs and the childlike unconsciousness of the dark face in which two eyes gleamed wide open as of those of a fearful little beast, impressed him unfavorably, and his heart, hardened by the daily spectacle of so many miseries, experienced a pious jolt at the sight of that little boy torn from his children's games and condemned, like so many unhappy creatures, to languish miserably in the humble galleries, next to the ventilation doors. The hard lines on his face softened, and with feigned harshness he told the old man that he was very anxious about the examination and fixed on him an anxious gaze:

–Man! This boy is still too weak for work. Is he your son?

–Yes, sir.

–You must have taken pity on his few years, and before you buried him here you should have sent him to school for some time.

–Sir –muttered the miner's rude voice in which an accent of painful supplication vibrated–. There are six of us at home and only one of us who works, Pablo is already eight years old and must earn the bread he eats and, as the son of miners, his trade will be the same of his elders, who never had any school other than the mine.

His opaque and trembling voice suddenly died out in a cough, but his wet eyes implored with such insistence that the foreman defeated by that mute plea brought a whistle to his lips and plucked from him a high-pitched sound that echoed far away in the deserted gallery. A rumor of hurried steps was heard and a dark silhouette was drawn in the doorway.

–Juan –exclaimed the little man, addressing the newcomer–, take this boy to the gate number twelve, he will replace José's son, the truck driver, crushed yesterday by the train run.

And turning abruptly towards the old man, who began to murmur a phrase of gratitude, he said to him in a harsh and severe tone:

–I have seen that in the last week you have not reached the five boxes, which is the daily minimum required of each hewer. Don't forget that if this happens again, it will be necessary to unsubscribe you so that another, more active worker can take your place.

And doing with his right hand an energetic gesture, he dismissed him.

The three of them left silently and the rumor of their footsteps gradually moved away in the dark gallery. They walked between two rows of rails whose sleepers sunk in the muddy ground, which they tried to avoid, lengthening or shortening their steps, guided by the thick nails that held the steel rods in place. The guide, still a young man, went ahead and further behind with the little Pablo in hand, the old man followed him with the beard plunged into his chest, deeply worried. The words of the foreman and the threat contained in them had filled his heart with anguish. For some time his decadence was visible to all; every day the fatal boundary which once passed through makes the old worker a useless piece of junk inside the mine drew nearer. Futilely, from dawn to night for fourteen deadly hours, turning like a reptile in the narrow labor, he attacked the coal furiously, fiercely against the inexhaustible seam, which many generations of forced men, as he, scratched unceasingly in the bowels of the earth.

But that tenacious and relentless struggle soon turned the youngest and most vigorous into decrepit old men. There, in the dark, humid and narrow burrow, their backs were bent and their muscles were loosened, and, like the rabid colt that trembles at the sight of the rod, the old miner felt their flesh shivering every morning at the contact of the vein. But hunger is more effective than the whip and the spur, and they taciturnity resumed the oppressive task, and the whole coal vein, riddled by a thousand parts by that human wood-worm, vibrated subtly, crumbling piece by piece, bitten by the quadrangular tooth of the beak, as the sandstone of the bank by the ravages of the sea.

The sudden detention of the guide pulled the old man out of his sad thoughts. A door closed their way in that direction, and on the floor close to the wall there was a small bundle, the contours of which were confusingly wounded by the flickering lights of the lamps: it was a ten-year-old boy huddled in a hole in the wall.

With elbows at the knees and a pale face between his gaunt hands, mute and motionless, seemed not to perceive the workers who crossed the threshold and left him again plunged into darkness. His eyes, opened without expression, were stubbornly fixed upwards, perhaps absorbed in the contemplation of an imaginary panorama that, like the mirage of the desert, attracted his pupils, thirsty for light, humid by the nostalgia of the distant glow of the day.

In charge of handling that door, he spent the endless hours of his imprisonment submerged in a painful self-absorption, overwhelmed by that enormous tombstone that advocated forever in him the restless and graceful mobility of childhood, whose sufferings leave in the soul that understands them an infinite bitterness and a feeling of acerbic execration for human selfishness and cowardice.

The two men and the child, after some time walking along a narrow corridor, ended up in a high dragging gallery from whose roof a continuous rain of thick drops of water fell. A dull, distant noise, as if a giant hammer were hitting the armor of the planet over their heads, was heard at intervals. That rumor, the origin of which Pablo was unable to explain, was the collision of the waves in the coastal breaks. They still walked a short distance and finally found themselves in front of the number gate twelve.

–Here it is –said the guide, stopping by the rotating blade of planks fastened to a wooden frame embedded in a rock.

The darkness was so thick that the reddish lights of the lamps, attached to the visors of the leather caps, barely gave a glimpse of that obstacle.

Pablo, who could not explain this sudden stop, contemplated his companions silently, who, after changing some brief and quick words among themselves, began to teach him with joviality and determination the use of the gate. The little boy, following his instructions, opened it and closed it repeatedly, dispelling the uncertainty of his father who feared that his son's strength would not be enough for the job.

The old man manifested his happiness, passing his calloused hand over the uncultivated hair of his first-born son, who had not shown tiredness or restlessness until then. His youthful imagination impressed by that new and unknown spectacle was stunned, disoriented. Sometimes it seemed to him that he was in a room in the dark and he thought he saw a window opening at every moment and the brilliant rays of the sun entering through it. And although his inexperienced little heart no longer experienced the anguish that assailed him in the downhill pit, those cuddles and caresses to which he was not accustomed aroused his distrust.

A light shone in the distance in the gallery and then there was the squeaking of the wheels on the road, while a heavy and fast trot made the ground rumble.

–It's the train run! –exclaimed the two men at the same time.

–Get ready, Pablo –said the old man–, let's see how you do your duty.

The little one, with clenched fists, leaned his tiny body against the gate which slowly gave way until it touched the wall. As soon as this operation was done, a dark, sweaty, panting horse quickly crossed in front of them, dragging a heavy train laden with ore.

The workers looked at each other satisfied. The rookie was already an experienced doorman, and the old man, leaning over his high stature, began to speak to him softly: he was no longer a child, like the ones up there who cry for nothing and are always clutching the skirts of women, but a man, a brave man, nothing less than a worker, that is, a comrade who had to be treated as such. And in short sentences he made him understand that they were forced to leave him alone, but he should not be afraid, for there were in the mine many others of his age, doing the same work; that he was near to him and would come to see him from time to time, and once the work was finished they would return home together.

Pablo heard it with increasing fright and as only answer he grabbed the miner's blouse with his hands. Until then he had not realized exactly what was required of him. The unexpected turn taken by what he thought was a simple walk produced an intense fear in him, and dominated by a vehement desire to leave that place, to see his mother and siblings, and to find himself again in the clarity of the day, he only answered his father's affectionate reasons with a moaning and fearful *"let's go!"* whiny and full of fear. Neither promises nor threats convinced him, and the *"let's go, Father"*, came from his lips more and more painful and urgent.

A violent setback was painted on the old miner's face; but when he saw those eyes filled with tears, desolate and begging, raised towards him, his nascent anger turned into an infinite piety: it was still so weak and small! And the paternal love asleep in the intimacy of his being suddenly recovered its overwhelming force.

The memory of his life, of those forty years of work and suffering was suddenly presented to his imagination, and with deep sorrow he found that from that immense labor he only had an exhausted body, which perhaps very soon they would throw out of the mine like a hindrance, and thinking that the same destiny awaited the sad creature, suddenly had an imperious desire to dispute his prey to that insatiable monster, who was tearing from the lap of mothers the barely grown children to turn them into those pariahs, whose backs receive with the same stoicism the brutal blow of the master and the caresses of the rock in the sloping galleries.

But that feeling of rebellion that began to germinate in him was suddenly extinguished before the memory of his poor home and of the hungry and naked beings for whom he was the only support, and his old experience showed him the senselessness of his chimera. The mine never let go any of those it had taken, and as new links replaced the old and worn ones, in an endless chain, down there the children succeeded the parents, and in the deep pit the going up and down of that living mark would never be interrupted. The little ones, breathing the poisoned air of the mine, grew rickety, weak, pale, but they had to resign themselves, for that is what they were born for.

And with resolute gesture the old man unrolled from his waist a thin and strong rope and in spite of the resistance and supplications of the child tied him with it in the middle of his body and immediately secured the other extremity to a thick bolt embedded in the rock. Pieces of string attached to that iron indicated that it was not the first time it had performed such a service.

The creature, half-dead of terror, uttered penetrating cries of dreadful anguish, and violence had to be used to tear it from between the legs of the father, whom he had grasped with all his might. Their prayers and cries filled the gallery, without the tender victim, more wretched than the biblical Isaac, hearing a friendly voice to stop the paternal arm armed against his own flesh, for the crime and iniquity of men.

His voices calling to the old man who was going away had such heartwrenching, deep and vibrant accents that the unhappy father felt his resolve waver again. But the fainting lasted only a moment, and covering his ears so as not to hear the screams that clutched his bowels, he hastened the march away from that place. Before leaving the gallery, he stopped for a moment, and listened: a faint voice like a breath was crying out far away, weakened by distance:

–Mother! Mother!

Then he ran like a madman, harassed by the wandering mourner, and stopped only when he found himself in front of the carbon vein, at the sight of which his pain suddenly turned into furious anger and, grasping the handle of his pick, he attacked it rabidly. On the hard block the blows fell like thick hailstones upon loud crystals, and the steel tooth sank into that black, shiny mass, tearing out huge pieces that piled up between the worker's legs, while a thick dust covered like a veil the flickering light of the lamp.

The sharp edges of the coal flew with force, wounding his face, neck, and bare chest. Threads of blood mixed with the copious sweat that flooded his body, that penetrated like a wedge in the open breach, widening with the eagerness of the prisoner that pierces the wall that oppresses him; but without the hope that encourages and strengthens the prisoner; to find at the end of the day a new life, full of sun, air and freedom.

Firedamp

In the entrance of the mine all movement had stopped. The wood workers smoked silently between the rows of empty wagons, and the chief foreman of the mine, a skinny little man whose shaven face, with protruding cheekbones, revealed firmness and cunning, waited standing with his lantern lit beside the stationary elevator. High above, the sun shone in a cloudless sky, and a light breeze blowing from the coast brought in its invisible waves the salty emanations of the ocean.

Suddenly the engineer appeared at the entrance door and stepped forward, the metallic plates of the platform resounding under his feet. He wore a waterproof suit and carried a flashlight on his right hand. Without deigning to answer the shy greeting of the foreman, he entered the cage followed by his subordinate, and a second later they disappeared quietly into the dark abyss.

When, two minutes later, the elevator stopped in front of the main gallery, the laughter, voices and screams that thundered that part of the mine ceased as if by enchantment, and a fearful whisper arose from the darkness and spread quickly under the dark vault.

Mister Davis, the chief engineer, somewhat obese, tall, strong, of rubicund physiognomy in which the *whiskey* had stamped his characteristic seal, inspired the miners an almost superstitious fear and respect. Hard and inflexible, his dealings with the workers ignored piety and in his racial pride he considered the life of those beings as a thing unworthy of the attention of a *gentleman* who roared in anger if his horse or dog were victims of the slightest omission in the care demanded by their precious existence.

The visits of inspection which, from time to time, were imposed on him by his position of chief engineer, were the black spot of his refined and sybaritic life. A fiendish humor took hold of his spirit during those tiring excursions. His irritability was translated into the application of punishments and fines that fell indistinctly on large and small, and his presence announced by the white light of his flashlight was more feared in the mine than the collapses and explosions of firedamp[1].

That day, as always, the news of his descent had produced some restless excitement in the various groups of workers. The workers fixed a suspicious gaze on each little light that shone in the darkness, believing to see at every instant that white and dreaded radiance appear. Everywhere they worked with feverish activity: the hewers, with their bodies shrunken, sometimes bent in implausible postures, ripped off, piece by piece, the crisp ore that the wheelbarrow operators drove pushing the squeaky wagons to the lathes of the hauling galleries.

The engineer stopped for a few moments with his companion, in the foremen's department where the first one informed himself of the details and necessities that had made his presence indispensable. After giving some orders there, always in company of the major foreman, he went towards the interior of the mine crossing tortuous corridors and very narrow passages full of mud.

Sitting on the flat side of a wagon from which the side woods had been removed, he occasionally made some observation to his subordinate who followed the wagon laboriously. Two boys with no other suit than cloth trousers, drove the singular vehicle: one pushed from behind and the other hooked like a horse pulled from the front. The latter showed great signs of tiredness: his body, flooded with sweat and the anguished expression of his countenance revealed the fatigue of excessive muscular effort. His chest swelled and depressed like a bellows on the impulse of his agitated respiration which escaped through his half-open mouth, hurried and longing. A kind of leather harness pressed his bare chest, and from the girdle around his waist two strings snapped to the front of the wagon. At the entrance of a passageway leading to the new works in operation, the chief whose attention was fixed on the cladding gave a loud voice, and directing the focus of his lantern upwards, he began to examine the leaks from the rock, chopping with a thin iron rod the wood that held the roof. Some of these beams had menacing curves and the rod penetrated them like if they were a soft, spongy thing. The foreman, with a restless look, contemplated in silence that examination, sensing one of those storms that so often exploded over his head of humble subordinate, abject and obsequious.

–Come here, come here. How long ago was this covering made?

–A month ago, sir –replied the troubled foreman.

---

1 Firedamp is flammable gas found in coal mines. It is the name given to a number of flammable gases, especially methane. It is particularly found in areas where the coal is bituminous. The gas accumulates in pockets in the coal and adjacent strata, and when they are penetrated, the release can trigger explosions.

The engineer turned and said:

–One month and the wood is already rotten! You're a clumsy man, you let yourself be cheated by the shorers that place soft wood in places like this one so saturated with humidity. You are going to take care of this damage before I make you pay dearly for your negligence.

The alarmed foreman retreated quickly and disappeared into darkness.

Mr. Davis supported the tip of the rod on the naked torso of the boy in front of him and the cart moved, but slowly because the slope made it very difficult to drag the cart on that soft and slippery ground. The one behind helped his companion with all his strength, but suddenly the wheels stopped turning and the wagon was still. The youngest of the drivers, his face in the mud, grasping the rails with both hands, as if he were still dragging the cart, lay still. In spite of his courage the fatigue had defeated him.

The voice of the chief whom the prospect of having to crawl folded in two on that waterlogged and dirty ground, put out of his mind, resounded angry in the gallery:

You scoundrel, you loafer! –he shouted in anger.

And the iron rod was raised and fell repeatedly, making a dull noise when it hit that inanimate body.

As he felt the blows, the fallen boy rose to his knees and, making an effort, rose to his feet. There was in his eyes an expression of rage, of pain and despair. With a nervous movement he stripped of his beastly harnesses and leaned against the wall where he stopped immobile.

Mr. Davis, who was watching him attentively, got out of the car and approached him with the rod in the air, saying:

–Ah! you're resisting, wait!

But seeing that the victim for all defense crossed his arms over his head, he stopped, was undecided for a moment and then with a toning voice said:

–Get out of here!

And turning to the other boy who trembled like a leaf on a tree, he commanded him imperiously:

–You, follow me.

And hunching over his tall stature, he continued onward through the gloomy gallery.

After hastily dispatching a crew of workers to carry out the repairs so harshly ordered on the cladding, the foreman went to wait for his boss at a small square bordering on the new works in operation, and was frightened to see him appear, after a long wait, with his face red, snorting with fatigue and sprinkled with mud from head to toe. He was so surprised that he did not take a step or make a gesture to approach his master, who, dropping himself heavily into some pieces of wood, began to shake his suit and wipe with his fine handkerchief the copious sweat that flooded his face.

The boy who came pushing the little cart, revealed in two words what had happened. The foreman listened to the news with restlessness and giving his physiognomy the most dismayed and tragic expression he knew, he approached his superior with a solicitous gesture; but the latter, understanding that this incident was ridiculous to his pride, had recovered the superb gesture of supreme disdain that was habitual to him, and nailing in the servile countenance of his subordinate the cold and implacable look of his grey pupils, he asked him with a seemingly serene voice, but with a certain dull irritation:

–Does this boy have relatives?

–No, sir –said the questioned man–, he has only a mother and three younger brothers: the father was crushed to death by a landslide when the work of the new tunnel began. He was a good worker –he added, trying to mitigate the son's fault with the father's merit.

–Well, you are going to give immediate order for this woman and her children to leave the room. I don't want idlers here –he say at last, with threatening severity.

His accent could not be replied to, and the foreman, bending one knee on the damp floor, took his notebook and pencil and drew some lines on it, by flashlight.

As he wrote, his imagination moved to the room of the widow and the orphans, and although those expulsions were frequent and as the executor of the master's unquestionable justice, sensitivity was not the vulnerable point of his character, he could not help but experience a certain unease over that measure which would cause the ruin of that miserable home.

At the end of the writing he ripped off the page and signaled to the boy to come closer to him, saying:

–Take it outside to the butler of rooms.

Chief and subordinate were left alone. In the small square that served as a deposit of materials, pieces of cladding wood, piles of rails and handles of picks, scattered around the black walls in which the even blacker openings of sinister passageways were drawn, were seen in the light of the lanterns.

A dull rumor, as of distant breakers, flowed through those hollows into short and intermittent waves: wheel squeaks, confused human voices, dry squeaks and a slow roll, impossible to locate, filled the massive vault of that deep cavern where darkness limited the circle of light to a very small radius behind which its compact masses were always on the lookout, ready to advance or retreat.

Suddenly, there at a distance, a light appeared followed by another and others until a few tens were completed. They looked like little red balloons floating in a sea of ink and going up and down following the undulating curve of an invisible wave.

The foreman took out his watch and said, interrupting the embarrassing silence:

–They are the hewers of the Half Sheet who come to deal with the question of the rebates. Yesterday they were summoned to this place.

And he went on to give meticulous details about the matter, details that his superior heard with clear displeasure, his eyebrows frowned and everything in him revealed growing impatience and when the foreman repeated his arguments for the second time he said:

–It is therefore impossible to increase the prices because, then, the cost of coal... –a rough and sharp "I know" cut him off abruptly.

The clerk sneaked a glance at his switch and a skeptical smile, invisible in the darkness, folded his thin lips as he distinguished the long row of approaching lights. It was not difficult to guess that the business of those poor hewers was in grave danger of becoming a disaster. And his conviction was affirmed by seeing the chief's grim frown and observing the traces that the walk through the gallery had left on his person and suit.

The knees of his trousers displayed large mud plates and his hands, ordinarily so white and well cared for, were those of a charcoal burner. There was no doubt, he had stumbled and fallen more than once. In addition, in his dented hat soot stains could be seen from the soot that the smoke from the lamps deposited on the roofs of the tunnels, which indicated that his head had verified practically the solidity of those coatings that had seemed so fragile to him. And as he progressed in that examination, a malignant joy was portrayed in the finely cunning countenance of the foreman. He felt avenged, even in part, of the humiliations which by the nature of his employment he had to endure daily.

The lights continued to draw near, and the rumor of voices and the splashing of the feet in the liquid sludge was already distinctly heard. The head of the column soon flowed into the square, and all those men lined up silently in front of the place occupied by their superiors. The smoke from the lamps and the pungent smell of their sweaty bodies soon permeated the atmosphere with a nauseating, asphyxiating stench.

And in spite of the considerable increase in light, the shadows always persisted and the blurred silhouettes of the workers were drawn on them, like confused masses of indeterminate and vague profiles.

Mister Davis was still on his stone bench, hands crossed on his thick abdomen, showing, in the gloom, the strong contours of his powerful musculature. A sepulchral silence reigned in the square, a silence that suddenly interrupted some old people's coughs, broken and hollow.

–Go ahead! what are you waiting for? Speak now! –exclaimed the engineer, addressing the foreman, who lifted the flashlight at the height of his head and projected a beam of light over the group from which a man stood out, advancing, cap in hand, and stopping three steps away.

Short in stature, with a sunken chest and pointed shoulders, his bald head, blackened as his face, upon which long strands of grey hairs fell, gave him a strangely laughable and grotesque appearance. A significant glance from the foreman gave him encouragement, and in a somewhat shaky voice he raised the question that had brought them together there: the matter was otherwise easy and simple. As the new vein only reached a maximum thickness of sixty centimeters, they had to dig four tenths more clay to accommodate the wagon. This additional work was the hardest part of the task, because the mineral was very consistent, and since the presence of the firedamp did not allow the use of explosives, the cut had to be deepened with picket blows, which demanded considerable fatigue and time. The small increase in the price of the wheelbarrow, setting it at thirty cents, was not enough, because although they began the task at dawn and did not leave the quarry until late at night, they could barely dispatch three wheelbarrows, and could count on the fingers of the hand those who raised that figure to four. And after making a sober picture of the misery of their homes and the hunger of wife and children, he ended up saying that only the hope that the reductions would make up for their hardships as they had been promised by being hired as the new vein hewers had sustained the strength of him and his comrades during that long fortnight.

The engineer heard that exposition, from the beginning to the end, without opening his lips, enclosed in a threatening silence that did not bode well for the interests of the applicants.

A grim silence followed for a few moments, interrupted by the slight crackling of the lamps and the occasional tenacious and recalcitrant cough. The group shuddered, their necks stretched and their ears sharpened. It was the shuddering voice of the chief who resounded, saying:

–How much rebate do you demand per meter?

That concrete and definite question was not answered. A murmur came from the ranks, and some isolated voices were heard, but they were immediately silent when they heard again the imperious voice which repeated in a sour tone:

–What's up! You don't answer?

The old man, who passed his cap from one hand to the other with indecisive air, thus directly questioned, took a step forward and said in a slow and insecure voice, trying to read on the veiled face of his interlocutor the effect of his words:

–Sir, it would be fair to be paid for every meter the price of four coal wheelbarrows because...

He didn't finish, the engineer had stood up and his obese person stood out taking on threatening proportions in the twilight nebula.

-You are insolent –he shouted in an angry voice– fools who believe that I am going to squander the company's money on fomenting the laziness of a herd of idlers who, instead of working, go to sleep like pigs in the corners of the galleries.

He paused to take a breath and added as if talking to himself:

–But I know the tricks and I know what the hypocritical lamentations of such scoundrels are worth.

And facing the foreman he instructed him, stressing each one of his words:

–Thirty cents shall be paid for the meter of cuttings in the Half Sheet to the hewers who extract on average four crates of coal daily. Those that do not reach this figure will only receive the price of the ore.

He was furious because, in spite of the economies introduced, coal was more expensive there than in the other seams, and the demands of the workers, who only confirmed that bad outcome, increased his resentment, since his prestige was endangered by the regrettable error of his calculations and forecasts.

Under their black masks the miners turned pale to lividity. Those words vibrated in their ears, echoing in the depths of their souls like the apocalyptic sound of the trumpets of the final judgment. A stupid expression, a stupor close to idiocy was painted on their dilated pupils, and their knees flinched as if the shadowy vault had suddenly sunk over them. But such was the fear that they had to the irritated and imposing figure of the master, and such was the dominion that his all-powerful authority, exercised over their poor spirits degraded by so many years of servitude, that no one made a move, nor let escape the slightest protest.

But then came the reaction, the despoilment was so enormous, the sorrow so hard, that their brains, stunned for a moment by that blow of a mallet, regained the consciousness of their acts. The first to recover the use of his faculties was the old man of the bald face who, seeing that the chief was about to leave, resolutely closed his step, saying with a mournful voice:

–Sir, have mercy on us, that what was promised is fulfilled, we have earned it with our blood. Look yourself!

Pulling out the sleeve of his blouse, he showed his left arm wrapped in dirty bandages, which he violently removed, revealing a deep tear that went from his collarbone to his forearm. That wound deprived of its dressing began to flow blood in abundance.

–Sir –he continued–, have pity on us, we beg on our knees.

But the engineer did not hear him, discussing busily with the foreman the shortest way to reach the new tunnel destined to connect the new works with the old ones.

A threatening murmur arose behind him as he set out, and the old man, seeing that he was leaving the square, in an access of despair reached out his hand and took him by the clothes.

A formidable arm was raised in the darkness and with a furious backhand he threw the daring one ten paces away. There was a thud, a whimper, and everything was silent again.

A moment later the boss and his companion disappeared at an angle in the corridor.

In the square, a scene worthy of the condemned of hell developed. In the gloom of the shadow the lights of the lamps were shaken, moving in all directions and terrible oaths and atrocious blasphemies sounded in the darkness, going to awaken along the walls the sadly gloomy echoes of the rock as insensible as the ferocious selfishness before that immense desolation.

Some had thrown themselves to the ground and dumb as inert masses remained astonished without seeing or hearing what was happening around them. An old man cried in silence, huddled in a corner, and his tears traced winding furrows in the coppery, wrinkled skin of his blotchy face. In other groups there was heated discussion and gesticulation, and the noise of the quarrel was interrupted at every moment by curses and roars of anger and pain. A tall, skinny boy with tense fists walked among the groups, hearing the different opinions, and convinced that there was no remedy, that the sentence dictated was irrevocable, in a furious rapture he crashed his lamp into the wall, where it was torn to pieces, and began to strike his head against the rock until he fainted at the foot of the wall.

Little by little the spirits calmed down and a chunky young man exclaimed aloud.

–I won't throw another pick stroke, may the devil take everything!

–It's very easy to say that when you don't have a wife or children –someone replied promptly.

–If we even could use gunpowder. Damn firedamp! –the one with the bald head complained.

–It would be the same thing, comrade. As soon as they saw that we were earning a little more, they'd lower our salaries.

–And you young men are to blame -said an old man.

–Oops, grandfather, stop saying that, you are going too far! –said the first one who had spoken.

–Yes –insisted the old man-, you and no one else is to blame because you burst working and make us all burst. If you measured your strength they wouldn't lower prices and this dog's life would be less hard.

–We just don't like to look at our hands when we're working.

–I didn't look at them either, and you see what I've got.

There was a moment of silence, and after a brief pause the deep, melancholic voice of the old man resounded again:

–I was also young, and like you I did the same; I mocked the old without thinking that youth passes so fast that when one notices it, one is already wasted, a piece of junk. I am old, but we must not forget that everyone is on that path; that death drives us and the one who stops has the penalty of life.

Everyone was silent again, and the old man who groaned in the corner got up and with a languid step left the small square.

Very soon the others followed his example, and in the depth of the gallery the flickering lights of the lamps again submerged themselves in those dark waves that in an instant drowned their fugitive and dying glow.

* * *

In the new tunnel the excavation work had been momentarily interrupted and there was only a crew of workers propping up the supports, three men and one boy. Two of them were busy sawing the timber and the other two were adjusting them in their places. They were already at the end and only a few meters away from the rock wall that was being drilled.

A worker and a boy were determined to place a piece of beam in an upright position: the first held it, while the second, with a heavy mallet, hit the top. Seeing the little success they obtained, they decided to remove it to shorten its length, but it was embedded so solidly that despite their efforts they could not achieve it. Then, they began to dispute with acrimony blaming each other for having mistaken the measure of the cut of that wood. After a bitter exchange of words they turned aside, sitting down to rest on the pieces of rock scattered on the ground.

One of the man who was cutting wood approached, examined the beam, and seeing the sign of blows near the roof, he said, addressing the boy:

–Be careful when you hit so high. One spark, one single spark, and we all will burn in this hell. Come here, come and see –he added, crouching at the foot of the wall.

–Put your hand here, what do you feel?

–Something like a little wind that blows.

It's not the wind, comrade, it's the firedamp. Yesterday we covered several cracks with clay, but this one escaped us. The gallery must be full of this bloody gas.

And to make sure, he lifted the safety lamp above his head: the light grew considerably longer, as soon he saw that, he lowered the lamp quickly.

–Devil! –he said –There's enough firedamp here to make the whole mine jump.

That boy whose age ranged from eighteen to nineteen was known by the singular nickname of Black Wind. Quarrelsome and boastful, with strong and resilient limbs, he abused his physical vigor with his companions, generally weaker than himself, for that reason he was little esteemed among them. In his pockmarked face, there was a firmness and resolution that contrasted notably with the timid and inexpressive faces of his comrades.

The worker and the boy went to continue their conversation sitting on a beam.

–You see –said the first–, we are, that is the case, inside the barrel of a shotgun, at the place where the load is placed, and pointing in front of him at the high tunnel, he continued: At the slightest oversight, a spark that jumps or a lamp that breaks, the Devil pulls the trigger and the shot comes out. As for those of us who are here, we would simply make the role of pellets.

Black Wind did not answer. At the top of the tunnel he saw the light of the engineer's lantern shining. The other ones, too, had seen it, and they both got up in a hurry and went on with the interrupted task.

The boy took the mallet and set out to hit the beam, but his companion prevented him from doing so, telling him:

–You don't see how useless that is!

–But here they come, and something must be done.

–I won't do anything until they arrive, and then I'll ask them to give me another helper, because you don't take care of my observations at all.

And again the discussion flared up, and they would have come to blows if the presence of his superiors had not prevented it. Chief and subordinate carefully examined the cladding, and very soon the foreman's watchful gaze was fixed on the beam which was the object of the dispute.

–What is this, Juan?

–It is his fault, sir –replied the worker, pointing to the boy–, he does as he pleases and does not obey my orders.

The foreman's penetrating eyes were stuck in Black Wind and he suddenly exclaimed in a threatening tone:

–Ah, it's you who cut the signal line of the foremen's department yesterday! You have a five pesos fine for the misdeed.

–It wasn't me! –roared the accused, pale of anger.

The foreman shrugged with indifference, but seeing the immobility of the worker and the furious look that gushed from his eyes, he shouted emphatically at him:

–What are you doing there, you lazy bastard? Quick, get that wood out of the way!

The boy didn't move. In his uneducated and indomitable soul, that fine so unjustly applied to him, produced on him the effect of a whipping, irritating to exasperation his fierce and resolute character.

The foreman, furious at that unusual ignorance of his authority, grabbed the disobedient by the neck and shoved him forward, ending his aggression with a violent kick from behind. He should never have done it! Black Wind revolved against him like a tiger and hitting him with a tremendous head blow in the middle of his chest, he thrust him limp on the hard floor.

The engineer who was taking notes in his briefcase near there, and who, noticing the dispute was preparing to intervene, turned when he heard the blow of the fall and perceiving a shadow sliding against the wall, jumped in front of him, closing his way. The fugitive wanted to escape on the other side, but an iron fist grabbed him by the arm and dragged him like a feather to the bottom of the tunnel.

Sitting on a stone, surrounded by the workers, the foreman turned from his temporary fainting breathing with difficulty. When he saw his aggressor he wanted to pounce on him, but a gesture from the engineer held him back.

–He has hit him with his head on his chest –said the workers, answering the chief's questioning gaze, who without letting go of his prisoner's arm led him in front of the beam and ordered him in a calm, almost friendly tone:

–Before anything else you're going to put that stand in place.

–I said I don't want to work –Black Wind replied with a dull, opaque voice.

–And I tell you that you will work, if the hammer isn't enough you can try with your head with which you are so skillful.

An explosion of laughter greeted the joke that made the disfigured face of the worker pale with rage; he turned his gaze of cornered beast around him, in which the dark flame of an indomitable resolution shone. And, suddenly, contracting his muscles, he leapt forward trying to pass through the free space between the engineer's body and the wall of the corridor. But a terrible punch that hit him in the face threw him on his back with extreme violence.

He got up leaning on his hands and knees, but a ferocious kick in his kidneys rolled him again through the rubble of the gallery. The witnesses of that scene followed his adventures breathless and eagerly.

Black Wind, full of mud, frightful, bloody, stood up. A thread of blood sprouted from his right eye and was going to be lost in the corner of his lips, but with a firm step he stepped forward and taking the mallet he began to discharge furious blows on the inclined beam.

A smile of satisfied pride shone across the wide face of the engineer. He had tamed the shrew and at every furious blow that made the wood slide on the rock he repeated placidly:

–Well, boy, bravo, well, well, well!

The foreman was the only one who perceived the danger, but only managed to stand up.

On the black roof a few sparks shone one after the other. Black Wind had let the handle of the mallet slide through his hands up to its extremity, and the steel mallet, when touching the sharp edges of the rock, had produced in them the fulminating effect of the collision of the steel against the flint.

A blue flame swiftly crossed the warped roof of the tunnel and the mass of air contained within its walls ignited, becoming an immense flame. The hair and the clothes burned, and a very vivid light, of extraordinary intensity, illuminated even the most hidden corners of the inclined gallery.

But that dreadful vision lasted only the very brief space of a second: a terrible crackle moved the bowels of the rock, and the six men were wrapped in a whirlwind of flames, pieces of wood and stones and projected with frightful violence along the corridor.

* * *

At the dull bursting of the formidable explosion, the inhabitants of the small hamlet crowded the doors and windows of their homes and fixing his dazed eyes on the constructions of the mine, witnessed full of fright something like the sudden eruption of a volcano.

Under the blue sky, serene and limpid, with no hint of smoke or flames, the beams of the hoist, plucked from their places by a prodigious force, were thrown upwards in all directions: one of the iron cages, running along the narrow tube of the well, like a projectile through the barrel of a cannon, climbed straight up to an immense height.

The inhabitants of the mining population, mostly women and children, rushed in a confused flock towards the entrance of the mine, where everything was confusion and disorder: the workers ran from one side to the other, terrified without finding what to do. But the presence of the foreman in charge reassured them a bit, and under his direction they began to work with feverish activity. The cages had disappeared, and with them one of the cables, but the other one was intact, wrapped up in the coil. Quickly a pulley was mounted over the mouth of the pit and by tying a wooden bucket to the end of the cable everything was ready for a descent. The foreman and two workers were already preparing to carry out this operation when a thick smoke that began to sprout from below impeded them, and they had to wait for the fans to sweep that obstacle.

In the meantime the maddened women had invaded the platform making the rescue work more difficult, and the workers had to reject them pushing and punching them, to clear the site of the maneuver. Their shrieks deafened the men, preventing them from hearing the command voices of foremen and machinists.

At last the smoke dissipated and the foreman and the workers were placed inside the bucket: they gave the sign of descent and disappeared in the midst of the deepest silence.

They left the improvised cage in front of the entrance gallery and entered inside. A terrifying calm reigned in that place, there was no ray of light and everything was clear of obstacles; there was no trace of wagons or wood; the pulleys, the cables, the signal cords, everything had been swept away by the violence of the air pushed by the explosion. That loneliness overwhelmed them, and a deadly anguish oppressed their hearts. Had all their companions died?

But suddenly a great number of lights appeared and they found themselves surrounded by a compact group of workers. As they felt the commotion they had hurriedly run towards the exit point, but as they emptied into the central gallery they had been stopped by the smoke and the breathless air that filled that part of the mine. They knew nothing of the workers at the entrance to the pit; no doubt they had been buried together with the rubble in the deepest part of the pit.

Opinions were in agreement that the explosion had taken place in the new tunnel and that the team of underpinners, the chief engineer and the chief foreman of the mine must have perished in it.

A unanimous cry resounded: Let's go! And they all got moving, but the foreman's loud voice stopped them:

–Nobody move –he said with authority–, the gallery is full of black wind. The first thing is to activate the ventilation. Close the floodgates of the second gallery so that the air of the ventilator works directly on the tunnel. Then we'll see what needs to be done.

While some rushed to execute those orders, the blacksmith Tomás, a tall and robust young man, approached him and with a resolute tone said:

–I will go there, if there is anyone who accompanies me. It is a cowardice to abandon one's companions in this way. Some of them still may be alive.

–Yeah, yeah! Come on! –exclaimed a score of voices.

The foreman tried to dissuade them, telling them that it was to run uselessly to an almost certain death. It was more than two hours since the explosion and therefore the chiefs and comrades were undoubtedly gone and well dead. But seeing that they did not listen to him, he agreed with the worker's proposition to avoid greater misfortune. After a violent dispute, because everyone wanted to be of the party, he chose three companions with whom he immediately set out.

At the entrance to the tunnel the four men knelt down and made the sign of the cross, and then, one after the other, with the lamps high, they entered the gallery, which by its elevation allowed them to walk straight without stooping. Very soon they felt their temples beating and ringing in their ears. A hundred yards away the one at the head felt a blow on his back: the worker following him had fallen. Without any waste of time they lifted him up and dragged him out. They replaced him quickly, and the small group went back into the corridor.

When they were a hundred meters from the end, they found the first body. A glance was enough for them to understand that it was impossible for him to keep a spark of life: he was in pieces. A few more steps and they stumbled on the second, then on the third, fourth and fifth. The last one was that of the foreman, who was recognized by his thick nailed shoes.

The engineer was missing, and without stopping they continued advancing, but suddenly in front of them there was a thick block that fell with great noise, raising a cloud of dust. They were at the site of the explosion; the ground was strewn with rubble, the coverings had been largely torn off, and the roof was beginning to give way. They stopped for a moment undecided, but then, passing over the obstacle, they went on, cautiously, with their ears attentive to the forerunners of the landslides and feeling at every step the sharp blows of some falling rocks. They walked a few meters when suddenly a cracking sound resounded. Tomás, who was the first of the group, received a blow on a shoulder that made him waver on his legs: he became full of anguish; a thick dust prevented him from seeing. He stepped forward cautiously and his teeth chattered: in front of him and shutting him out, there was a pile of stones more than a meter high spanning the entire width of the gallery. He jumped over that tomb and began to remove the rubble furiously, a task which was soon seconded by his companions who arrived, but after great efforts they found only three corpses.

While some collected the dead, the others searched the corners in search of the engineer whose strange disappearance awakened in their superstitious spirits the idea that the Devil had taken him away in body and soul.

Suddenly someone shouted:

–Here it is!

They all came and illuminated with their lamps. At one corner of the gallery, glued to the ceiling and on the axle intended to hold the cable pulley, at the end pointing to the bottom of the tunnel, there was a large suspended bulge. That bulky mass that gave off a penetrating smell of burnt flesh was the body of the chief engineer. The tip of the thick iron bar had penetrated his belly and protruded more than a meter between his shoulders. With the horrible violence of the crash, the bar had been twisted and it took a great deal of work to get him out of there. When the body was removed, as the clothes turned into hot ash were undone at the slightest contact, the workers stripped off their blouses and covered the body with them piously. In their rough souls there was no hint of hatred or rancor. As they set out with the stretcher on their shoulders, they breathed with fatigue under the crushing weight of the dead man who was still gravitating upon them, like a mountain on which the humanity and the centuries had piled pride, selfishness and ferocity.

Payday

Pedro María, with his legs shrunk, lying on his right side, traced a cut in the lower part of the vein with the help of a pickaxe. That incision that the hewers call circa[1] already reached to thirty centimeters of depth, but the water that filtered through the ceiling and ran by the block filled the furrow every five minutes, forcing the miner to release the tool to extract with the aid of his cap of leather that dirty and black liquid that, draining under his body, was going to form big ponds in the bottom of the gallery.

He had been working hard for a few hours to finish that cut and begin the task of removing the charcoal. In that very narrow mousetrap the heat was unbearable. Pedro María was sweating profusely, and from his body, naked up to his waist, a warm mist sprouted, which, combined with the smoke of the lamp, formed around him a kind of fog whose opacity, prevented him from seeing with precision, and made the hard and interminable task more difficult. The scarce ventilation increased his fatigue, the air loaded with impurities, heavy, asphyxiating, drowned him and caused him suffocation accesses, and the height of the work, about a scarce seventy centimeters, only allowed him to take uncomfortable and forced postures that ended up numbing his limbs causing him intolerable pains and cramps.

Leaning on his elbow, with his neck bent, he beat without rest, and with each stroke the water of the cut whipped his face with thick drops that wounded his pupils like hammer blows. Then he stopped for a moment to drain the furrow and took up again the pickaxe without taking care of the

---

1 CIRCA: Perforation that is made in the floor of the coal vein to facilitate its extraction.

fatigue that engulfed his muscles, or the unbreathable atmosphere of that hole, nor of the mud in which his body was sinking, harassed by a fixed, obstinate idea, to extract that day, the last of the fortnight, the greatest possible number of wheelbarrows; and that obsession was so powerful, it so absorbed his faculties that physical torture caused in him the effect of the spur that tears the flanks of a runaway horse.

When the circa was finished, Pedro María, without allowing himself a minute of rest was ready immediately to release the mineral. He tried several postures, looking for the most comfortable to attack the block, but had to resign himself to continue with the one he had adopted until then, lying on his right side, which was the only one that allowed him to handle the pickaxe with relative ease. The task of pulling out the coal, which to a novice would seem very simple, requires no little skill, because if the blow is very oblique the tool slides, releasing only small pieces, and if the inclination is not enough, the steel tooth bounces off and stands out as if it were marzipan.

Pedro María began the task with ardor, he attacked the coal next to the cut and, knocking from top to bottom, large black and shiny pieces were detached from the vein, which quickly piled up along the cleft; but as the blow went up, the work became very painful. In that small space the necessary impulse could not be given to the pickaxe: narrowed between the ceiling and the wall, it bit the block weakly, and the worker, desperate, multiplied the blows removing only small pieces of ore.

A very copious sweat soaked his body, and the thick dust that came out of the vein, mixed with the air that he breathed, entered his throat and lungs producing coughing accesses that tore his chest, leaving him breathless. But he beat, he beat ceaselessly, fiercely against that obstacle that he would have wanted to tear apart with his nails and teeth. And furiously, enraged, at the risk of being buried there, he ripped from the ceiling a large plank against which the tool crashed at every moment.

A drop of water, persistent and quick, began to fall at the base of his neck, and his fresh contact seemed delicious at first; but the pleasant sensation soon disappeared to become a burn-like sting. In vain he tried to dodge that leak which, having previously slipped through the wood, was going to get lost in the wall and which was now burning its flesh as if it were melted lead.

However, he did not give up with his tenacious determination, and while the coal crumbled piling up between his legs, his eyes searched for the right place to poke that wall that he had been piercing for so many years, which was always the same, so thick that the end was never seen...

Pedro María left the job at dusk and taking his lamp and dragging himself painfully along the corridors, he won the central gallery. The currents of air that he found in the passage had cooled his body, and he walked broken and in pain, hesitating on his legs hindered by so many hours of forced immobility...

When he found himself outside on the platform, an icy blow whipped his face, and without stopping, he quickly descended down the road. Over his head large masses of dark clouds ran, pushed by a strong wind from the north, in which the silvery disc of the moon, thrown in the opposite direction, seemed to penetrate with the violence of a projectile, paling and eclipsing among the dense clouds and re-emerging again, fast and bright, through a fugitive tear. And before those furtive appearances of the moon, the darkness fled for a few moments, revealing out the bright spots of the ponds on the dark floor, that the worker did not take care to avoid in his haste to arrive soon and to find himself under a roof, next to the beneficent flame of the home.

With his clothes stuck to his skin, he entered the narrow room. Some coals burned in the chimney, and in front of it, hanging from a string, were a pair of trousers and a blouse of canvas, clothes that the worker put on without delay, throwing the wet ones in a corner. His wife then spoke to him, complaining that she had not got anything in the company store that day either. Pedro María did not answer, and as she continued to explain to him that night he had to go to bed without having supper, because the little coffee they had was destined for the next day, her husband interrupted her, telling her:

–It doesn't matter, woman, tomorrow is payday and our sorrows will end.

And with his limbs shattered by fatigue, he went to lie down on his bed, leaning against the wall. That bed composed of four boards on two benches and covered by a few sacks, had nothing but a frayed and dirty blanket. The woman and the two boys, a five-year-old child and an eight-month-old baby, slept in a similar bed, but more comfortable, as a straw mattress had been added to the sacks.

During those last five days since the office cut off their provisions, the scarce clothes and utensils had been sold or pawned; for in that remote place there was no other store of provisions than that of the Company, where all were obliged to buy with vouchers or tokens to the bearer.

Very soon a heavy sleep closed the eyelids of the worker, and silence reigned in those four walls, interrupted at times by the gusts of wind and rain that scourged the doors and windows of the miserable room.

Pedro María woke up quite late in the morning. It was one of the last days of June and a fine and persistent drizzle fell from the dark grey and ashy sky. On the side of the sea a thick curtain of mists closed the horizon, like an opaque wall that advanced slowly, swallowing in its path everything that the sight perceived in that direction.

Under the zinc of the corridors, between the coming and going of the women and the crazy races of the children, the workers, with their chests bare, rubbed each other's skin spiritedly to get rid of the soot acquired in a week of work. The day destined to the payment of wages was always awaited with anxiety and in all the faces shone a certain joy and animation.

Pedro María, having finished his weekly washing, stood for a moment leaning against the door frame, looking vaguely at the plain and contemplating silently the tenacious and monotonous rain that soaked the blackish soil, full of potholes and dirty ponds. He was a man of barely thirty-five years of age, but his emaciated face, sunken eyes, gray beard and hair made him look more than fifty.

For him, the sad and fearsome era in which the miner sees the courage and energies of his ephemeral youth weaken, along with his physical vigor had already begun.

After having contemplated for a moment the sad landscape that unfolded before his eyes, the worker entered the room and sat down next to the chimney where in the iron bowl the water for coffee was already boiling.

The woman, who had gone out, returned, bringing bread and sugar for breakfast. Younger than her husband, she already looked old and withered by that life of work and deprivation which the nursing of the little one had made more difficult and painful.

At the end of the petty snack, husband and wife began to calculate the sum that he would receive as payment and, rectifying again and again their accounts, they came to the conclusion that after paying the company store they had enough left over to rescue and buy the utensils that need had forced them to get rid of. That prospect made them happy, and as at that moment the bell of the paying office began to ring, the worker put on his shoes and followed the woman who, carrying one creature in her arms and the other small one clinging to her hand, walked sinking her bare feet in the mud, headed towards the road, joining the numerous groups that were rushing away in the direction of the mine.

The strong wind and rain forced them to accelerate their steps to seek refuge under the sheds surrounding the entrance of the mine, which later became insufficient to contain that motley crowd.

There were all the personnel involved in the various tasks, from the old foreman to the eight-year-old doorman, holding tight between them to avoid the water running from the eaves of the roofs and with their eyes fixed on the closed window of the payer.

After waiting for a while, the window shutter rose, and the payment of wages began immediately. This operation was done by sections, and the workers were called one by one by the foremen who guarded the small opening through which the cashier was delivering the amounts that constituted the credit of each one. These sums were generally reduced, as they were limited to the balance remaining after deducting the value of the oil, coal and fines and the total of what was purchased from the company store.

The workers approached and withdrew in silence, because it was forbidden to make observations and no claim was attended to, but when the last worker had been paid. Sometimes a miner paled and fixed a look of surprise and fright in the money placed at the edge of the window, without daring to touch it, but one imperative word from the foremen: get out, made him stretch out his hand and pick up the coins with his trembling fingers, then he turned away with his head down and a stupid expression on his disturbed countenance.

His wife came out to meet him anxiously, asking him:

–How much did they give you?

And the worker would answer by opening his hand and showing the coins, and then they would look into each other's eyes, becoming dumb, overwhelmed, and feeling the earth falter beneath their feet.

Suddenly some laughter interrupted the religious silence that reigned there. The cause of that untimely noise was a miner who, seeing that the employee was putting a single twenty-cent coin on the tablet, took it, looked at it for a moment with attention like a curious and strange object, and then threw it with anger away from himself.

A mob of small rascals lunged like lightning after the coin that had fallen, raising a slight splash in the middle of a pond, while the worker with his hands in his pockets went down the road without heeding the voices of a poor old woman who, with her skirts raised, ran screaming with an anguished accent:

–Juan, Juan! –But he did not stop, and very soon his gaunt figures, whipped by the wind and the rain, disappeared, dragged away by the torrent never exhausted by pain and misery.

Pedro María waited patiently for his turn and when the foreman exclaimed out loud:

–Hewers from the Double! –he shuddered and waited nervously, his ear attentive to his name being pronounced, but the three words that constituted it did not reach his ears. One after the other his companions were called, and when he heard again the high-pitched voice of the foreman shouting:

–Half-Leaf Hewers! –A shiver ran through his body and his eyes grew large. His wife turned and said to him, between surprised and fearful:

–They haven't called you, look! –and as he did not respond she began to groan, while rocking in her arms the little one who bored of sucking the exhausted breast of the mother had started to cry desperately.

A neighbor approached:

–They haven't called you yet?

And as the questioned woman shook her head negatively, she said:

–She pointed at his son, a twelve-year-old boy, but so pale and rickety that he didn't look more than eight.

That woman, a young widow, tall, well formed, with a graceful face, red lips and very white teeth, leaned against the wall of the shed and from there threw gleaming glances at the window behind which the blond whiskers and the incarnated cheeks of the payer could be seen.

Pedro María, meanwhile, tortured his head doing calculations after calculations, but the worker like so many others who were in the same case did the math without the guest, that is, without the unforeseen fine, without the reduction of the salary or the sudden and capricious increase of the prices of the company store.

When the last worker of the last section had approached the window, the foreman's harsh voice resounded clear and vibrant:

–Claims!

And a hundred men and women rushed to the office: all of them were animated by the hope that a forgetfulness or an error was the cause of their names not appearing on the lists.

In the front row was the widow with her boy holding her hand. He brought his face closer to the opening and said:

–José Ramos, doorman.

–Has he not been called?

–No, sir.

The cashier went through the pages of the book and read in a brief voice:

–José Ramos, 26 days at twenty-five cents. He has a fine of one peso. He owes fifty cents to the office.

The red woman of rage replied:

–A fine of one peso! Why? And it's not twenty-five cents he earns, but thirty-five!

The clerk did not deign to answer, and with an imperious and urgent tone shouted through the window:

–Another!

The young woman wanted to insist, but the foremen pulled her out and pushed her violently out of the circle.

Her energetic nature revolted, her rage suffocated her and her gazes gave off flames.

–Scoundrels, thieves! –she shouted after a moment in a crooked voice. With his head thrown back, his body erect, standing out beneath the wet clothes, his broad shoulders and his curved bosom encircled, she was poised for a moment in an attitude of challenge, throwing rays of intense anger through his dark and slanting eyes.

–Don't be mad, woman, you offend God! –Someone mocked among the mob.

The questioned one became furious like a lioness.

–God! –For the poor there is no God!

She looked furiously at the window, and she exclaimed:

–Cursed, without conscience, the earth will swallow them up!

The foremen smiled from underneath and their eyes shone greedily contemplating that true female. The widow glanced defiantly at everyone and turned towards her boy, who with an open mouth looked intoxicated at a band of seagulls flying in a row, his plumage standing out under the misty sky, like a white ribbon that the wind was pushing towards the sea, she shouted at him, giving him a shove:

–Come on, beast!

The impulse was too strong and the little one's legs were so weak that he fell on his face into the mud. Seeing his son on the ground, the mother's nerves lost their tension and a crisis of tears shook her chest. She bowed quickly and lifted the boy, kissing him lovingly, and drying with his lips the tears that ran down those pale cheeks to which the poverty of blood gave a livid and sickly dye.

It was Pedro María's turn and he waited restlessly by the window. As the cashier turned the pages, his heart beat hard and the anguish of uncertainty narrowed his throat like a noose, so that when the paymaster turned and said to him:

–You have a fine of ten pesos for five faults, and twelve wheelbarrows have been deducted from your account. So you owe three pesos to the office.

He wanted to answer and could not, and he moved away from there with his arms down, walking awkwardly like a drunkard.

A glance was enough for the woman to guess that the worker had empty hands, and she began to weep, babbling, as she squeezed the creature convulsively in her arms:

–Holy Virgin, what are we going to do!

And her husband said to her, before she could ask him anything:

–We owe three pesos to the company –the unhappy woman doubled her cries, which the two little ones soon chorused. Pedro María contemplated that mute and somber desperation, and life appeared to him at that moment with characters so odious that if he had found a quick way to get rid of it, he would have done that without hesitation.

And through the open window a breath of misfortune seemed to flow: all those who approached that hole parted from him with a pale and convulsed faces, fists clenched, mumbling curses and oaths. And the rain always fell, copious, incessant, soaking the earth and piercing the clothes of those miserable ones for whom the drizzle and the inclemency of the sky were a very small part of their works and sufferings.

Pedro María, taciturn, with his eyebrows set close together, saw his wife and children go away, with even a more miserable appearance because their wets rags adhered to their flaccid flesh. His first impulse had been to follow them, but the quick vision of the naked and cold walls of the room, of the extinguished home, of the boy asking for bread, nailed it in place. Some companions called him making expressive winks, but he did not want to drink; his head weighed like lead on his shoulders and in his empty brain there was not an idea, nor a single thought. An immense laxity hindered his limbs and having found a dry place he lay down on the ground and very soon a heavy sleep full of extraordinarily strange and fantastic images and visions closed his eyelids.

And he dreamed that he was down there, pick in hand, attacking the vein, and strange thing, it seemed to him that the dark mass, brittle like glass, did not have the consistency of other times. He shook the lamp to see better and its strangeness disappeared. It was not coal or any other mineral the substance that the steely tip of his tool wounded, but a reddish, soft, gelatinous mass. Then he felt a vivid clarity penetrate his brain: that was the sweat, blood, and tears shed by generations of miners, his ancestors, in the corridors of the mine, and by those who still populated its infernal passageways. And without astonishment he saw that the sweat that flowed from his body was purple in color and that little by little he was taking on the dye and consistency of the extraordinary vein.

Then the vision was transformed and he found himself in front of an immense crucible where the strange mineral was thrown and that let escape by an opening of its lower part a golden water jet that jumped like a waterfall, spreading in golden streams by the fields.

At the contact of gold, the earth trembled and, like the blow of a magic rod, palaces and splendid dwellings sprouted from its bosom in whose resplendent rooms, like the day, innumerable couples intertwined in the rhythm of voluptuous dances.

Suddenly the dances and the music ceased and a strange, very rare light illuminated the rooms. The diamonds that shone in the hair and throats of the women detached from their settings and rolled like tears over the snowy shoulders and breasts of the beautiful ones, making them tremble with their wet contact. The rubies left bloody spots on the royal tapestries when they fell. And the walls, the staircases, the bronzes and the marbles, taking a red, violet, horrible dye, looked like coagulated blood.

While Pedro María was contemplating that abrupt transformation, a frightful mob rushed over the buildings: they were skeletons that with their hooked fingers tore apart those temples of fortune and pleasure, tearing off pieces that adhered to their bones turned into shreds of throbbing flesh.

As the skeletons were dressed in that strange way, acquiring blood and muscles, the palaces vanished shattered by those thousands of pliers and steel hooks. Nothing was left of the superb dwellings, nor the foundations. And when the last rubble, the last stone, had disappeared, only a crowd of old and young men and children, blackened and dirty, remained in that place.

The worker awoke suddenly. The sheds were deserted, and raindrops hummed their cheerful symphony, squeezing quickly over the eaves of the roofs.

The Devil's Pit

The original title of this tale is "El Chiflón del Diablo". It was the real name given to one mine by the miners that worked there for decades until the exploitation of coal was no longer profitable there.
"Chiflón" means "draught of air", but also is used to indicate the mine's tunnel. The draught of air may be appreciated when one gets close to the main pit of the mine.

In a low, narrow room, the foreman sitting at his desk with a large open register in front of him watched the workers descend on that cold winter morning. Through the doorway one could see the elevator waiting for its human load, which, once complete, disappeared with it, quietly and quickly, through the humid opening of the mine.

The miners arrived in small groups, and as they took down their lamps, already lit, from the hooks attached to the walls, a clerk fixed on them a penetrating glance, drawing with the pencil a short line at the margin of each name. Suddenly, on the way to the exit door, two workers were hastily stopped with a gesture, saying to them:

–You stay.

The workers became surprised and a vague restlessness was painted on their pale faces. The youngest, a boy in his early twenties, freckled, with abundant reddish hair, to whom he owed the nickname Copper Head, by which everyone designated him, was short, strong and robust. The other taller, somewhat skinny and bony, was already old, weak and ailing in appearance.

With their right hand, both of them held their lamps and with their left hand their bunch of small pieces of string in whose extremities buttons or glass beads of different shapes and colors had been tied; they were the chips or signs that the hewers put inside the charcoal wheelbarrows to indicate their origin when they were moved out of the mine.

The bell of the clock hanging on the wall gave slowly the six. From time to time a gasping miner rushed through the door, unhooked his lamp, and in the same haste left the room, casting a timid glance at the foreman as he passed by the table, who, without detaching his lips, impassive and severe, marked the name of the straggler with a cross.

After a few minutes of silent waiting, the employee beckoned the workers to come closer, and said to them:

–You're the wheelbarrow operators for the High, aren't you?

–Yes, sir –answered the questioned ones.

–I'm sorry to tell you that you're out of a job. I have orders to reduce the staff of that vein.

The workers did not answer, and for a moment there was a deep silence.

At last the oldest one said:

–But will the company give us jobs somewhere else?

The clerk closed the book tightly and leaning back on the seat, answered in a serious tone:

–I see it difficult, we have plenty of people in all the tasks.

The worker insisted:

–We accept the work that is given to us, we will be winch operators, shorers, whatever you want.

The foreman shook his head negatively.

–I have already said, there are plenty of people, and if the orders for coal do not increase, we will also have to reduce exploitation in some other veins.

A bitter, ironic smile contracted the miner's lips, and he exclaimed:

–Be frank, Don Pedro, and tell us once and for all that you want to force us to go and work at the Devil's Pit.

The employee stood on the chair and protested indignantly:

–No one is forced here. Just as you are free to refuse the work that do not like it, the Company, for its part, is within its right to take the measures that best suit its interests.

During that philippic, the workers listened in silence with their eyes down and when he saw their humble appearance the foreman's voice sweetened.

–But although the orders I have are strict –he added–, I want to help you get ahead. In the new tunnel, or in Devil's Pit, as you call it, are two vacancies for hewers, you can fill them right now, because tomorrow would be late.

A glance of intelligence crossed among the workers. They knew the tactics and knew beforehand the result of that skirmish: By the way, they were already determined to follow their destiny. There was no way to escape. Between starving to death or being crushed by a cave-in, the latter was preferable: it had the advantage of speed. And where to go? Winter, the implacable enemy of the helpless, like a creditor who falls on the assets of the insolvent without giving him truce or waiting, had stripped nature of all its finery. The warm rays of the sun, the glazed greenery of the fields, the dawn of rose and gold, the blue mantle of the heavens, everything had been taken away by that inexorable Shylock who, carrying in his right hand his immense bag, was gathering in it the treasures of color and light which he found on the face of the earth.

The storms of wind and rain that turned the languid brooks into torrents left the fields desolate and barren. The lowlands were immense ponds of swampy water, and on the hills and slopes of the mountains, the leafless trees flaunted under the eternally opaque sky the nakedness of their branches and trunks.

In the huts of the peasants, the hunger showed its pale face through the countenances of the people, who were forced to knock on the doors of the workshops and factories in search of the piece of bread that the wilted soil of the exhausted countryside denied them.

It was therefore necessary to surrender to fill the gaps that the fateful tunnel constantly opened in its ranks of helpless and defenseless workers, in perpetual struggle against the adversities of luck, abandoned by all, and against whom all injustice and iniquity was permitted.

The deal was done. The miners accepted their new work without further objection, and a moment later they were in the cage, plummeting into the depths of the mine.

The Devil's Pit had a sinister fame. Opened to give way to the ore of a newly discovered vein, the works had initially been executed with the required care. But as the rock deepened, it became porous and inconsistent. The leaks that were somewhat scarce at the beginning had been increasing, making the stability of the roof very precarious, although it was supported by solid coverings.

Once the work was finished, as the immense quantity of wood that had to be used in the shoring increased the cost of the mineral in a considerable way, this essential part of the work was neglected little by little. It was always clad, yes, but with weakness, economizing as much as possible.

The results of this system were not long in coming. It was necessary to continuously extract from there a bruised one, a wounded one and also sometimes some dead one crushed by a sudden detachment of that roof without enough support, and that, treacherously mined by the water, was a constant threat for the lives of the workers, who frightened by the frequency of the cave-ins began to shun the work in the deadly corridor. But the Company very soon overcame its repugnance with the bait of a few more cents in wages and salaries. The exploitation of the new vein continued.

Very soon, however, the increase of the wages was suppressed without paralyzing the work, being enough to obtain this result the method put in place, used by the foreman that morning.

Many times, in spite of the capital invested in that section of the mine, it had been thought of abandoning it, because the water soon spoiled the planks that had to be continuously reinforced, and although this was done only in the indispensable parts, the consumption of wood was always excessive. But to the misfortune of the miners, the coal extracted from there was superior to that of the other veins, and the flesh of the docile and tame herd placed in the lightest dish, balanced the scale, allowing the Company to exploit without interruption the very rich vein, whose black crystals kept through the centuries the irradiation of those millions of suns that traced their celestial route, from the east to the sunset, there in the childhood of the planet.

That night Copper Head arrived to his room later than usual. He was serious, meditative, and answered with monosyllables the affectionate questions that his mother asked him about his work of the day. In that humble home there was a certain decency and cleanliness often uncommon in those shelters where men, women and children were confused in disgusting promiscuity, along with such a variety of animals that each of those rooms suggested in the spirit the biblical vision of Noah's Ark.

The miner's mother was a tall, thin, white-haired woman. Her very pale face had a sweet, resigned expression that softened the glow of her wet eyes, where tears always seemed ready to slide. Her name was María of the Angels.

Daughter and mother of miners, terrible misfortunes had aged her prematurely. Her husband and two sons were killed one after the other by the sinking and the explosions of the firedamp, they were the tribute that their kind had paid to the insatiable greed of the mine. She only had that boy left for whom his heart, still young, was continuously startled.

Always afraid of a misfortune, her imagination did not depart for a moment from the darkness of the carboniferous mantle that absorbed the existence of who was her only treasure, the only bond that held her to life.

How many times in those moments of recollection had she thought, without being able to understand it, about the reason for those odious human inequalities that condemned the poor, the greatest number, to sweat blood to sustain the luxury of the useless existence of a few! And if only one could live without that perpetual anxiety for the fate of the loved ones, whose lives were the price, so many times paid, for the daily bread!

But those thoughts were fleeting, and not being able to decipher the enigma, the old woman chased away those ideas and returned to her chores with her usual melancholy.

As the mother gave the last touches to the preparations for supper, the boy sitting by the fire remained silent, abstracted in his thoughts. The old woman, worried by that silence, was preparing to interrogate him when the door turned on its hinges and a woman's face appeared through the opening.

–Good evening, neighbor. How is the sick man? –asked affectionately María of the Angels.

–The same than before –answered the questioned woman, entering into the room. The doctor says that the leg bone has not yet been welded and that it must be kept in bed without any movement.

The newcomer was a young woman with a dark countenance, emaciated by vigils and privations. She had on her right hand a tin-leaf basin, and as she answered, she struggled to divert her sight from the soup that smoked on the table.

The old woman stretched out her arm and took the jug, and as she emptied the hot liquid into it, she continued to ask:

–And did you speak, daughter, with the chiefs? Have they given you any help?

The young woman murmured with discouragement:

–Yes, I was there. They told me that I had no right to anything, that they did enough to give us the room; but, that if he died I should go and get an order to receive four candles and a shroud from the company's store.

And with a sigh she added:

–I hope in God that my poor Juan won't force them to make that expense.

María of the Angels added a piece of bread to the soup and put both gifts in the hand of the young woman, who made her way to the door, saying gratefully:

–The Virgin will repay you, neighbor.

–Poor Juana –said the mother, going to her son, who had put his chair next to the table–, it will soon be a month since they took her husband out of it with a broken leg.

–What did he do?

–He was a hewer at the Devil's Pit.

–Oh, yes, they say that those who work there have their lives sold!

–Not so much, mother –said the worker–, and now it's different. It's been more than a week since there have been any misfortunes.

–It will be like you say, but I couldn't live if you worked there; I'd rather go and beg in the fields. I don't want them to bring you a day like they brought your father and your brothers.

Thick tears streamed down the pale face of the old woman. The boy kept silent and ate without looking up from the plate.

Copper Head left the next morning for his work without informing his mother of the change of job from the day before. There would always be plenty of time to give her that bad news. With the carelessness of age he did not give much importance to the fears of the old woman. Fatalist, like all his comrades, he believed that it was useless to try to escape the destiny that each one had been assigned beforehand.

When one hour after the departure of her son María of the Angels opened the door, she was delighted by the radiant clarity that flooded the fields. It had been a long time since her eyes had seen such a beautiful morning. A nimbus of gold surrounded the disc of the sun that rose above the horizon, sending torrents of its vivid rays over the humid earth, from which bluish and white vapors flowed everywhere. The light of the sun, soft as a caress, poured a breath of life on the still life. Flocks of birds crossed, far away, the blue and serene sky, and a cock of iridescent feathers, on the top of a mound of sand sounded a strident alert each time the shadow of a bird slipped by his side.

Some old men, leaning on sticks and crutches, appeared beneath the filthy corridors, attracted by the glorious glow that illuminated the landscape. They walked slowly, stretching their numb limbs, eager for that warm heat that flowed from on high.

They were the invalids of the mine, the vanquished of the work. Very few were those who were not mutilated and who were not lacking an arm or a leg. Sitting on a wooden bench that received the full rays of the sun, their pupils, fatigued, sunk in the orbits had a strange fixity. Not a word crossed between them, and from time to time, after a brief, cavernous cough, their closed lips half-opened to give way to a spittle as black as ink.

The hour of noon was approaching and in the rooms the busy women prepared the baskets of snacks for the workers, when the brief ringing of the bell made them leave their work and to precipitate terrified outside the rooms.

In the mine the ringing had ceased and nothing foreshadowed a catastrophe. Everything there looked ordinary, and the chimney let loose, without interruption its enormous plume which widened and grew dragged by the breeze which pushed it towards the sea.

María of the Angels was busy placing the bottle of coffee in the basket destined for her son, when she was surprised by the alarm and, releasing those objects, she rushed towards the door in front of which they were escaping, with their skirts raised, groups of women followed closely by mobs of little children who were desperately running after their mothers. The old woman followed that example, her feet seemed to have wings, the sting of terror galvanized her old muscles, and her whole body shook and vibrated like the string of the bow at its maximum tension.

Soon she was in the first row, and her white head, wounded by the rays of the sun seemed to attract and precipitate behind her the shady mass of the ragged flock.

The rooms were deserted. Their doors and windows opened and closed with a clatter of wind. A dog tied up in one of the corridors, seated on his hindquarters, his head turned upward, let a dreary howl be heard in response to the mournful cry that reached him, extinguished by the distance.

Only the old men had not left their sun-heated bench, and mute and motionless, they always remained in the same attitude, with their shady eyes fixed on an invisible beyond and oblivious to anything but that fierce irradiation that infiltrated their bodies with a little of that energy and that warm heat that made life grow again on the deserted fields.

Like the chicks who, suddenly perceiving the rapid descent of the sparrow hawk, rush desperately to seek refuge under the mother's bristly feathers, those groups of women with their hair unraveled, who whimpered whipped by terror, soon appeared under the hoist's stark arms, pushing each other and pressing together on the damp platform. The mothers squeezed their little children, wrapped in dirty rags, against the half-naked breasts, and a clamor that had nothing humane sprouted from their half-open mouths contracted by pain.

A strong barrier of timber defended the opening of the well on one side, and part of the crowd was stopped there. On the other side a few workers with a sullen, silent and taciturn gaze, contained the tight rows of that mob that deafened them with their screams, asking for news of their relatives, the number of dead and the place of the catastrophe.

At the door of the machine departments one of the engineers, a corpulent Englishman with red sideburns, appeared with a pipe between his teeth, and with the indifference that custom gave him, he glanced over that scene. A formidable imprecation greeted him and hundreds of voices howled:

–Murderers, murderers!

The women raised their arms above their heads and showed fists drunk with rage. The one who had provoked that explosion of hatred threw a few puffs of smoke into the air, and turning his back, disappearing back into the machine's departments.

The workers' news of the accident calmed the excitement somewhat. The event did not have the proportions of the catastrophes of other times: there were only three dead, whose names were still ignored. For the rest, and there was almost no need to say it, the misfortune, a collapse, had occurred in the Devil's Pit gallery, where the workers had already been digging for two hours to extract the victims, the winch operators were waiting from one moment to the next for the signal to lift the men.

That story gave birth to hope in many hearts devoured by restlessness. María of the Angels, leaning against the barrier, felt that the tongs that bit her insides loosened her iron hooks. It was not her hope but certainty: surely he was not among those dead. And concentrating on herself with the ferocious selfishness of mothers, she heard almost indifferently the hysterical sobs of other women and their woes of desolation and anguish.

Meanwhile the hours fled, and under the arcades of lime and brick the motionless machine let its iron limbs rest in the gloom of the vast chamber; the cables, like the tentacles of an octopus, emerged shuddering from the deepest bite and twisted their flexible and viscous arms into the coil; the tight and compact human mass throbbed and groaned like bleeding and dying cattle, and above, over the immense countryside, the sun, already crossed the meridian, continued throwing the sparkling beams of its warm rays, and celestial calm and serenity fell from the concave mirror of the sky, blue and diaphanous, which did not tarnish a cloud.

Suddenly the women's crying ceased, a bell followed by three others resounded slow and vibrant: it was the signal to hoist. A shudder shook the crowd, which eagerly followed the oscillations of the cable going up, at the end of which was the terrible unknown that everyone longed for and was afraid to decipher.

A mournful silence barely interrupted by one or other sobbing reigned on the platform, and the distant howl spread across the plain and flew through the air, wounding hearts like an omen of death.

Some moments passed, and suddenly the big iron ring that crowned the cage appeared over the rim. The elevator swung for a moment and then was stopped by the hooks on the upper flange.

Inside it some workers with bare heads surrounded a black wheelbarrow, dirty with mud and coal dust.

An immense clamor greeted the appearance of the funereal chariot, the crowd swirled and their mad despair made it very difficult to remove the corpses. The first one to appear to the avid glances of the mob was lined with blankets, barefoot, stiff, and mud-stained. The second man who immediately followed the previous one had a bare head: he was an old man with a beard and grey hair.

The third and last one appeared in turn. Between the folds of the fabric that enveloped it there were some locks of red hair that threw to the light of the sun a reflection of newly melted copper. Several voices uttered in horror:

–The Copper Head!

The corpse taken by the shoulders and by the feet was laboriously placed on the stretcher that awaited it.

When María of the Angels perceived that livid face and that hair that seemed soaked in blood, she made a superhuman effort to pounce on the dead body; but pressed against the barrier, she could only move her arms while an inarticulate sound gushed from her throat.

Then her muscles loosened, her arms fell along the body and she remained motionless in place as if wounded by lightning.

The groups moved away and many faces turned to the woman, who with her head bent over her chest, immersed in absolute sensitivity, seemed absorbed in the contemplation of the abyss opened to her feet.

A ray of light, passing through the network of cables and wood, would obliquely illuminate the humid wall of the pit. Attracted by that bright white point, the pupils of the old woman, frightfully dilated, nailed themselves into the luminous circle, which slowly and as if obeying her inexorable, scrutinizing gaze, was widening and penetrating into the mass of rock as if through a transparent, diaphanous crystal.

That slit, similar to the tube of a colossal telescope, placed in the sight of María of the Angels an unknown world; a labyrinth of corridors opened in the living rock, submerged in impenetrable darkness and in which the ray of the sun scattered a vague and diffuse clarity.

Sometimes the beam of light, like a barrier of diamonds, pierced the roofs of gloomy galleries, which were followed by inextricable networks of narrow passages through which a varmint could barely slide.

Suddenly the pupils of the old lady were encouraged: there was a long, steep corridor in sight in which three men were struggling to place a wheelbarrow of ore inside the track. A heavy rain fell from the roof on their naked torsos. María of the Angels recognized her son as one of those workers, the instant they stood up violently and fixed in the roof a look of fright, a dry snap followed and the vision disappeared.

As the darkness dissipated, the old woman saw a dense cloud of dust floating on a pile of rubble, at the same time as a call of infinite anguish, a cry of terrible agony rose through the immense acoustic tube and murmured beside her ear:

–My goodness!

* * *

It was never known how she crossed the barrier. Stopped by the cable levels, she was seen for an instant to shake her legs in the void, and then, without a shout, disappear into the abyss. A few seconds later, a dull, distant, almost imperceptible noise erupted from the hungry mouth of the pit from which puffs of faint vapors escaped: it was the breath of the blood-bearing monster at the bottom of his den.

The Well

With her arms rolled up and carrying on her head a bucket full of water, Rosa crossed the free space between the rooms and the small orchard, whose near branches and dry trunks stood out dark, almost black, in the sandy soil of the dusty countryside.

The dark-skinned, glowing ascetic face of the girl had all the freshness of being sixteen and the soft, warm coloration of the fruit not yet touched. In his green eyes, shaded by long eyelashes, there was a carefree and picaresque expression, and his mouth of red and sensual lips showed when laughing two rows of white teeth that a queen would envy.

That posture, her arms held high, made her firm, round and inciting breasts stand out in the opulent bust slightly thrown back and under the coarse cloth bodice. As she walked, the flexible waist and the undulating blue percale skirt modeled her hips indicating a shapely and strong female.

Soon she found herself in front of the gate that gave access to the fenced area and penetrated into it. The vegetable garden, very small, was planted with vegetables whose welted and withered squares the young woman began to refresh with the water she had brought. Turning back toward the entrance, she plunged in the bucket placed on the ground, both hands, and threw the liquid with force in front of her. Absorbed in this operation she did not realize that a man, slipping stealthily by the open shutter, advanced towards her at a wolf's pace, avoiding making any sound. The newcomer was a very young man whose pale, almost impervious face was illuminated by two dark eyes full of fire.

A slight fuzz marked his upper lip, and the straight black hair that fell on his tight, narrow forehead gave him an almost childish appearance. He wore a T-shirt with white and blue stripes, grey trousers, and he donned hemp espadrilles. The slight rubbing of the dry leaves that covered the floor made the young woman turn quickly, and an expression of surprise and marked disgust was painted in her expressive face.

The visitor stopped in front of a square of cabbages and lettuces that separated him from the girl, and stood still, devouring her with his gaze.

The girl, with low eyes and a frown, kept silent wiping her hands in the folds of her skirt.

–Rosa –said the young man in a cheerful and smiling tone, which revealed a badly contained emotion– how you turned around in time. What a scare I would have given you!

And changing his accent with a passionate and insinuating voice, he continued:

–Now that we are alone you will tell me what you have been told about me; why don't you listen to me and hide when I want to see you.

The questioned woman remained silent and her air of contrariness was accentuated. The amorous reclamation became tender and pleading.

–Rosa –the voice implored–, am I so unlucky that you despise my affection, this heart that is more yours than mine? Remember that we were engaged, that you loved me!

With a concentrated accent, without looking up from the floor, the girl answered:

–I never told you anything!

–That's true, but you didn't dodge when I was talking to you about love either. And the day I swore to marry you, you didn't say no to me. On the contrary, you laughed and you said yes with your eyes.

–I thought you were joking.

A forced smile wandered across the lips of the gallant and in a tone of painful reproach he replied:

–A joke! Look! Even if they laugh at me because I'm getting married without sampling the merchandise, say a word and right now I'm going to look for the priest to give us the blessings.

Rosa, whose impatience and annoyance had been increasing, bowed down for only answer, took the bucket and took a step towards the door.

The young man moved, cutting her off, and in a dark and resolute tone exclaimed:

–You're not leaving here until you tell me why you've changed your opinion of me!

–I have nothing to say to you, and if you don't let me pass, I will shout and call my mother.

A wave of blood colored the boy's pale face, a flash of lightning erupted from his eyes and in a trembling voice from the pain and anger he uttered:

–Ah, bitch, I know who made you this way, but before he gets away with it, as there is a God, I will tear out his tongue and soul! Rosa, standing in front of him, contemplated him harshly and sullenly.

–For the last time, do you want to be my wife or not?

–Never! –said the young woman fiercely. First dead!

The look with which she accompanied his words was so contemptuous and there was such an expression of defiance in his green and luminous pupils that the boy was stunned for a moment without finding anything to answer; but suddenly, drunk with resentment and desires, he jumped towards the girl, took her by her waist and lifted her up in the air, knocking her down on the leaf litter.

A very violent struggle took place. The young woman, robust and vigorous, put up a desperate resistance and her teeth and nails were stuck with fury in the hand that suffocated her cries and prevented her from demanding help.

An unexpected apparition saved her. A second individual stood at the doorway. The aggressor leapt up with clenched fists and with a sparkling gaze awaited the intruder who advanced straight towards him with a frowned face and bloodshot eyes.

Rosa, her cheeks burning, furrowed with tears of fire, repaired the disorder of her clothes, standing next to the fence. The tears of her bodice showed treasures of hidden beauties that her owner insisted on covering with the scarf knotted around her neck, embarrassed and weeping.

Meanwhile, the two young men were waging a fight to the death. The first furious and rabid onslaught revealed their vigor and skill as fighters. The defender of the girl, also very young, was a hand higher than his antagonist. With wide shoulders and a beefy chest, he was a good-looking man with light eyes, curly hair and blond whiskers. Silent, with no weapons but fists, his eyes cast flashes of hatred under the arch of his contracted eyebrows, he attacked with extraordinary fury. The shortest one, of thin limbs, dodged with astonishing agility the terrible punches that his enemy was delivering to him, hitting him back punch by punch, firm and straight on his steel shanks. Their gasping breath whistled as it passed through the clenched teeth that gnashed with rage whenever the fist of the adversary reached their congested and sweaty faces.

Rosa, while tearing out with her fingers the dry leaves adhered to the very black waves of her hair, followed with her flaming eyes the vicissitudes of the scuffle, which continued without visible advantages for the enraged champions, who in front of the maiden redoubled their attacks like wild beasts in zeal that disputed the possession of the female that excited and made them fall in love with her.

The squares of vegetables were trampled mercilessly and that destruction started a look of desolation to the angry eyes of the young woman. The anger that burned in her chest increased, and the instant her offender passed her, harassed by his formidable adversary, she had a sudden inspiration: she bent down and, taking a handful of sand, threw it to his face. The effect was instantaneous, the retreating one stopped hesitantly and in a second he was knocked down on the ground where he remained motionless, his chest pressed under the victor's knee.

Rosa cast a last glance at the group, and then, without worrying about the empty bucket, she rushed out of the fence and raced the distance that separated her from her rooms. When she arrived she turned to look back and distinguished among the bushes the figure of her savior who was moving away, while on the opposite side the vanquished was walking, leaving the battle site in a hurry.

The young woman slid down the almost deserted corridors and after passing a series of doors, stopped in front of a barely ajar one and, pushing it gently, crossed the threshold. A large fire burned in the chimney and in the middle of the room a woman squatted in front of a wooden trough, washing some pieces of clothing. The bleached and bare walls indicated the misery of the place. On the floor and thrown into the corners there was rubbish which exhaled an unclean smell. A table and some chairs made up all the furniture, and behind the door there was a handrail from a staircase leading to a second room in the upper floors. The old woman, mature, corpulent, with a face covered in freckles and spots, without interrupting her work, fixed a scrutinizing gaze on the girl, suddenly exclaiming strangely:

–What happened to you?

Rosa, with a mournful and tearful tone, replied:

–Oh, mother! The garden is in pieces, the cabbages, the lettuces, the radishes, everything has been pulled up and trampled underfoot!

The woman's countenance turned red like purple.

–Ah, damned –she shouted– surely you have left the door open and the pig has entered from the other side.

She stood waving her rolled arms rolled up above her elbow and unleashed herself in insults and threats.

–You rascal! If that's the case, get the leather ready because I'm going to rip it out of you.

And with the skirts up she hastened to verify the disaster.

The atmosphere was heavy and hot and the sun rose to the zenith in a slightly misty leaden sky. In the grey and shifting sand their feet sank, leaving a whitish furrow. Rosa, who was walking behind her mother, throwing restless and scrutinizing glances everywhere, distinguished after an instant, above a small bush, the head of someone on the lookout.

The young woman smiled. She had just recognized the one who was her defender, who, seeing that the girl had discovered him, sat up a bit and sent her a kiss with his right hand across the distance. The girl's eyes shone and her cheeks stained with carmine, and in spite of understanding that, given the violent character of her mother, perhaps a beating awaited her, she cheerfully, almost smilingly penetrated the maladjusted orchard inside which rose a formidable chorus of groans, curses and oaths.

* * *

Rosa belonged to a family of miners. An only child, she helped her mother with household chores, while her father, an old hewer, struggled fiercely beneath the earth to earn the miserable wage that was her daily bread. The girl, coarse and rustic, was quite a beauty. Nothing innocent, because the environment did not allow it. She had, however, a harsh virtue, inaccessible until then to the seductions of the gallants who drank the winds of that beauty, with a healthy body, exuberant of life, showing the irresistible grace of the woman already formed.

Among those who most closely besieged her, two handsome and gallant young men who were the flower and cream of the lady killers of the mine were distinguished. Both had put the beautiful Rosa under siege; she received his passionate statements with laughter, affected ways and pouting full of grace and malice. Friends since childhood, love had cooled their relationships, ending up separating them completely.

For some time, Remigio the wheelbarrow operator, a pale dark young man, thin and slender, seemed to have inclined to his favor the very little interest that the disdainful girl lent to her adorers. But it was short-lived, and the young man in love saw with bitter disappointment that the hewer Valentín, his blond rival, was displacing him in the fickle heart of the beautiful girl. She, who at first smiled at his passionate protests, sometimes encouraging him with an inflammatory look, suddenly began to run away from him, to avoid his presence, and the few occasions he managed to speak to her, the girl would barely utter out one or another evasive phrase, accompanied by a gesture of detachment and displeasure.

The wench's deviation exalted his passion to the infinite. Bitten by jealousy, he doubled his efforts to regain the lost ground, crashing against the growing lack of love of the young woman who every day showed with visible signs his sympathy and preference for the other one. Their rivalry increased and the hatred nestled in the rivals' hearts made them two irreconcilable enemies. They watched each other and made use of every means at their disposal to hinder the other one and prevent him from taking any advantage.

As always and according to the custom, the siege put by the gallants to their daughter did not disturb in the least the parents. Whether or not she gave in to the loving claim, it was a matter that only concerned her. Remigio, the scorned suitor, wanted one day to have a decisive explanation with the young woman and to come out, once and for all, of the uncertainty that tormented him, for which he decided to skip his work at the bottom of the quarry one morning. Valentín, who was informed by a comrade of that novelty, suspicious of the reason that caused it, decided to stay to spy on the steps of his rival, which brought as a consequence the encounter of the orchard and the terrible combat that followed.

Rosa, whose heart was still asleep, had welcomed with a certain coquetry the loving insinuations of Remigio, who was the first one to request her. The conquest that had aroused the envy of many of her companions was flattering; but the vehemence of that love and the gaze of those dark eyes that were fixed on hers loaded with passion and desires made her tremble. The fear of man, of the male, appeased, then, the emerging ardor of his flesh, producing an instinctive feeling of repulsion in the proximity of the boy.

But when the other one, the blond and handsome Valentíne, began to court her, a sudden change took place in her. She blushed when she saw the young man, and if he spoke to her, the incisive, lively and prompt answer with which she knew how to keep the most daring gallants away, would not come out of her lips; instead, after babbling one or the other monosyllable, she ended up slipping away, confused and blushing.

The open and frank physiognomy of the boy, his cheerful and turbulent character, attracted her unconsciously, and the love hidden until then
in the bottom of his being germinated vigorously in that virgin land.

After the scuffle of that day the attitude of the two rivals changed.
While Valentín continued to court the girl openly, Remigio limited himself
to watching her at a distance. His passion excited by jealousy and stung by
spite had turned into a voracious bonfire that consumed him. His exalted
imagination forged the wildest plans to take revenge, prompt and terrible,
of the infidel, the traitor.

Rosa, for her part, fully devoted to her nascent love, did not take much
care of her former suitor. She did not hold a grudge against him and for him
she only had a disdainful indifference.

Things stayed that way for some time. The garden had been repaired
and the vegetable squares redone, but the authors of the destruction were
never discovered nor was it known what had happened there.

One day the girl's father had a bright idea, since water for irrigation
had to be carried from a great distance, he decided to open a well next to
the fence. When he told his wife and daughter about the project, they ap-
plauded him warmly. There were no great difficulties to overcome, for the
land on which the small town was settled was made up of black, coarse sand
to great depth. The water flowed only four meters from the surface, and
kept the same level in all seasons. It was agreed that the following Sunday
the work could be done for. Some friends offered their help, among the
most enthusiastic being Remigio and Valentín.

The designated day arrived and the work began very early in the
morning. The excavation was made near the entrance door and at noon
had been deepened to two meters. The sand was extracted by means of a
great bucket of iron tied to a cord that passed through a pulley, attached to
a wooden crossbar.

The adversaries were the most persistent in the task, but always avoiding all contact. While one was downstairs filling the bucket, the other was
upstairs pushing the sand away from the opening. At a moment when
Remigio was stuck in the hole, Valentín, pretending that he was thirsty,
threw the shovel and headed straight for Rosa's room. The young woman
was sitting sewing by the door.

–I came to ask you for a glass of water. I'm thirsty –said the worker, in
a cheerful and malicious tone.

Rosa got up in silence, her eyes shining and going to a corner of the
room she came back with a glass that Valentín took along with the little
brown hand that was holding it.

The smiling, blushing young woman uttered:

–Go on, don't spill it!

He looked at her smiling, fascinating her with his gaze. He drank the
water from a sip and then, wiping his lips with the sleeve of his blouse,
added, festive and flattering:

–Rosa, if I had to drink a glass of water every minute to see you, I
would swallow the sea.

The young woman laughed, showing off her white teeth.

−And it is so salty!

−Like that, and with fish, boats and everything!

With a cheerful laugh the girl greeted the occurrence.

−Wow, what a swallower!

A voice asked from above:

−Rosa, who's there?

−It's Valentín, mother.

An exclamation indicating indifference passed through the ceiling and everything was silent.

Valentín had taken the girl by the waist and pulled her towards himself. The girl, not collaborating, with his hands on the boy's wide chest, resisted and murmured in a pleading, silent voice:

−Leave me alone!

His warped bosom filled up like the swell on a stormy day, and his heart struck her inside with accelerated and dizzying hammering.

The fiery boy said to her tenderly:

−Rosa! My life! My beautiful dove!

The young woman, defeated, fixed on him a faint glance, full of promises, impregnated with passion. The rigidity of her arms loosened little by little, and as she felt the breath that burned his face approaching, she retreated, throwing back his beautiful head until she touched the wall. Then she closed her eyes, and the boy with his hungry mouth gathered the fresh mouth placed within his reach, the first fruits of those lips more ardent than a bunch of carnations and sweeter than the honeycomb elaborated in the fronds by the wild bee.

A heavy step that made the staircase creak caused the lovers to move away abruptly. The worker left the room saying aloud:

−Thank you, Rosa, see you later!

The agitated, trembling young woman picked up the needle again, but her pulse was trembling and pricked herself at every moment.

Valentín, as he walked towards the well, had his thoughts filled with joy, hoping that the final triumph was near. If the lovers' opportune occasion presented itself, the rustic beauty would be his. His experience as a seasoned gallant gave him certainty, and he could not help but cast a triumphant glance at Remigio when one of the companions said to him with derision:

−How was the water, did you quench your thirst?

Twisting, his blond mustache he replied sententiously:

−God knows more and asks less.

At dusk the well was finished. It was four meters deep and two meters in diameter, and from the bottom of it the water gushed slowly. The workers moved away from there and went to the shadow of the corridor to prepare the wooden framework designed to prevent the fragile walls of the excavation from collapsing. Remigio stayed for a moment to fix a flaw in the pulley and when the mending was over he was going to continue after his companions. The vision of Rosa's blue skirt, seen through the branches of the fence, made him change his determination and, taking the rope, he slipped into the hole.

The young woman, who had not seen him, was going to take some vegetables for a snack and thought to take a look at the work and see if the water began to rise.

Remigio, standing close to the humid wall, waited quietly and motionless. Rosa cautiously approached the edge of the opening and looked inside. The boy's presence surprised her, but then a mischievous smile appeared on her lips. She stretched out her hand, grabbed the rope whose upper end was tied to a stake, and jerked the bucket up to the pulley and held it there, rolling up the rest of the rope in one of the supports of the crossbar.

The worker did not try to prevent that maneuver. He had managed to perceive the young woman's fleeting face as she leaned down, and that joke seemed to him a favorable symptom in her rebuffed situation. He looked up and waited impatiently for the result of the trick.

Suddenly he heard a drowned exclamation and something like the rumor of a fight came to interrupt the silence of that mute scene. He straightened up as if he had seen a snake and, sharpening his ear, he began to listen with all his soul. A harmonious voice, soft as a complaint, murmured halfhearted and pleading phrases, and a deeper and more manly one answered with a passionate and ardent whisper.

The noise seemed to move away in the direction of the orchard, the shutter closed with a crash, the dry leaves cracked like the soft bed and spring that receives its nightly charge, and the sound was extinguished.

Remigio turned pale as a dead man, his muscles twitched and his teeth gnashed with rage. He had recognized Valentín's voice and with a wild rage turned like a tiger into the well, knocking his fists against the damp walls and directing upward glances maddened by rage and despair.

Suddenly he felt the blade of a very sharp dagger tear his flesh. A light scream, as fast as the flapping of a bird, had crossed over him. All his blood rushed to his heart, his eyes fogged and a red flame dazzled him.

And while through the warm and suffocating atmosphere slipped the caressing and rhythmic symphony of the fiery and interminable kisses, Remigio inside the hole suffered the tortures of hell. His fingernails were nailed to his chest until the blood flowed and the piece of blue sky that he perceived from below reminded him of the vision of clear, limpid and deep eyes whose pupils, humid by the divine drunkenness, would reflect in that instant the image of other eyes that were not his dark and gloomy own eyes.

At last the hinges of the door squeaked and a quick whisper followed by the snap of a kiss wounded the ears of the prisoner, who a moment later felt the footsteps of someone stopping at the edge of the cavity. A shadow was cast on the wall and a mocking voice uttered from above an ironic and bloody phrase that was a deadly injury.

A roar escaped from Remigio's chest, he paled intensely, and his gleaming eyes measured the distance separating him from his offender who, laughing, unleashed the rope and let it slide down the pulley.

The prisoner's first impulse was to rush out in pursuit of his enemy, but a sudden fainting prevented it. After he recovered, he was going to undertake the ascent when a slight trepidation of the ground produced by a horse that, pursued by a dog, passed at gallop near the opening, made detach some pieces of the walls and the sand went up to near his knees, burying the bucket of iron. The fear of perishing buried alive without being able to quench his rabid thirst for revenge gave him strength, and as agile as an acrobat he climbed up the rope and found himself outside the excavation.

Once free, he was left for a moment undecided as to the course he should follow. The plain stretched monotonously around him, deserted under the sky of a pale blue that the sun tinged with gold in its flight to the horizon. The atmosphere was one of fire, and the sand burned like the embers of an immense furnace. A hundred steps away, the white rooms of the workers rose, surrounded by small orchards protected by palisades of dry branches.

What a sum of work and patience each of those enclosures represented! The earth, carried from a great distance, was spread in light layers over that infertile soil like a precious material whose conservation sometimes caused disputes and bloody quarrels.

Remigio, prey to an infinite sadness, glanced through the landscape and found it gloomy and grim. The horse, whose step near the well had been about to produce a sinking, galloped far away, raising clouds of dust under his hoofs. But the memory of the received offenses soon overcame, in the boy, the dejection, and the sting of vengeance awoke in his uneducated and half-barbaric soul the implacable fury of his wild passion.

No torment seemed enough to him for those who had so cruelly mocked his loving desire, and he swore not to forgive any means of revenge. Engulfed in these thoughts he made his way late into the rooms. Although love had turned into hatred, he felt a sharp desire to meet the young woman to inquire in her face, so loved before, the traces of the caresses of the other.

Very soon he crossed the empty space between the well and the first orchards. On that feast day, in the midst of the women and children, the men came and went along the corridors with the cloth trousers fastened by the leather belt and the cotton T-shirts attached to their wide and strong chests. Joyful voices, shouts and laughter, the barking of a dog and the desperate crying of some creature were heard everywhere.

In front of Rosa's room, Rosa's father and several workers worked hard on the wooden armor that had to support the walls of the excavation. Remigio stopped at the angle of a fence from which he could see what was happening in the room of the young woman, who in front of the door, with her bare arms turned up to her elbow, twisted some pieces of clothing that she was extracting from a bucket placed on the floor. Valentín, leaning on the lintel in a conqueror's posture, addressed her phrases that found in the girl a happy and pleasant echo. Her fresh laughter ran like a dart through the heart of Remigio, since her happiness only increased the anger boiling in his chest. In the young woman's face there was a gleam of joy, and her wet pupils had an expression of passionate languor that increased their brightness and beauty.

When the last piece of cloth had been squeezed, Rosa took the bucket and went to one of the fences followed by Valentín, who carried a roll of string on his right hand. The blond strong boy tied the ends of the rope to the protruding ends of two pieces of wood, helping immediately to suspend the clothes from it. Without guessing that they were spied on, they continued their loving conversation sheltered from the glances of those who were in the corridor, when Valentín perceived twenty steps away, glued to the fence, the threatening figure of his rival and wanting to make him feel all the weight of the defeat and the fullness of his triumph, he surrounded the neck of the young woman with his left arm and, throwing his head back to her, kissed her on the mouth. Then he spoke mysteriously to her ear.

Remigio, who looked at the scene with a grim glance, saw the young woman turn to him quickly, look down at him and then burst out with a loud laugh. Then she let go of the arms that were holding her, and ran, laughing madly.

The offended boy was as good as stuck in place. His face felt hot and reddened to the root of his hairs. Blinded by courage he advanced a few steps staggering like a drunkard.

Going towards the well, Valentín walked, singing an insulting couplet:

> The fool who falls in love
> He's a complete fool
> He works and heats the water
> For someone else to take the mate[1].

Remigio, with a blank expression, followed him. There was only one thought in his brain: kill and die, and in the paroxysm of his anger he felt strong enough to attack a giant.

Valentín had stopped at the edge of the excavation and pulled the rope to make the bucket rise, but seeing that the sand that covered it made his efforts useless, slid to the bottom to free it from that obstacle. When Remigio saw it disappear he stopped for a moment, disoriented, but then a sinister smile appeared on his lips and walking faster he approached the opening and untied the rope, which slipped through the pulley and fell into the hole. The worker straightened up: his enemy was imprisoned and could not escape him. But how to finish him off? His eyes then scanned the ground looking for a weapon, a stone, and stopped in the tracks of the horse, which suddenly awoke in him a memory, a distant idea. Ah if he could throw ten, twenty horses on that shifting terrain! And to his overexcited spirit came strange ideas of vengeance, of tortures, of atrocious torments. Suddenly he shuddered. A thought as fast as lightning pierced his brain. Fifty yards from there, behind one of the orchards there was a small square where a hundred workers were entertaining themselves in various games of chance: throwing the dice and playing cards. He heard their voices distinctly, their screams and laughter. There he had what he needed and in a few seconds he devised and matured his plan.

The day declined, the shadows of the objects grew longer and longer to the east when the players saw Remigio appear in front of them, with his arms held high in a gesture of supreme consternation, shouting in a stentorian voice:

---

1 Infusion of *yerba mate* that is usually taken alone and occasionally accompanied with medicinal or aromatic herbs.

–The well collapses! The well collapses!

The workers turned in surprise, and those who were lying on the ground stood abruptly like a spring. And they all nailed their eyes to the boy, and none of them moved, but when they heard him repeat again:

–The well has collapsed! Valentíne is inside!– they understood, and that human avalanche, fast as a spout, rushed towards the excavation.

Meanwhile, Valentín, ignorant of the danger he was in, had extracted the bucket, which, because it was not necessary there, had been claimed by Rosa's mother. The fall of the rope did not cause him any surprise and he blamed it on the impotent resentment of his rival whose steps he had felt upstairs, but he was not alarmed because of it because from one moment to the next they would come to place the wooden armor and he would be freed from his prison. But when he heard the distant clamor and the phrase "the well collapses" came distinctly towards him, the sting of fear and the threat of danger made his heart shrink. The crowd came like an avalanche. The worker looked up in terror and watched with horror as pieces of the walls fell away.

The sand slid like a thick black liquid that piled on the bottom and went up along his legs.

He gave a terrible cry. The ground was suddenly shaken, and a bundle of heads, forming a narrow circle around the opening, eagerly leaned down.

A hoarse scream escaped from Valentín's throat.

–For God's sake, brothers, get me out of here!

The sand reached his chest and, like water in a container, it kept going up intermittently, slowly and silently.

Around the well the crowd grew by the minute. The workers were piling, squeezed, anxious to see what was going on downstairs. An immense vociferous sound thundered the air. The most contradictory orders were heard. Some asked for ropes and others shouted

–No, no, bring shovels!

Under Valentín's arms there had passed a cord which those above pulled with fury; but the sand did not release its prey, it retained it with invisible tentacles that adhered to the victim's body and held him with its wet and terrible embrace.

Some old workmen had made futile efforts to drive away the greedy multitude whose treading would only precipitate the catastrophe. The cry, "The well is collapsing", had left the rooms empty. Men, women, and children ran despondently to that place, unknowingly contributing to Remigio's sinister plan, who, with his arms folded, fierce, and somber, contemplated at a distance the success of his stratagem.

Rosa struggled in vain to get close to the opening. Her penetrating cries of anguish resounded above the general clamor, but no one took care of her despair and the barrier that closed her path became more impassable and tenacious at every moment.

Suddenly there was a movement in the mob. A dishevelled, terrified old woman harrowed the living mass that was silently separating to give way. A groaning came out of her chest:

–My son, son of my soul!

She reached the edge and without hesitation rushed into the hole. Valentín cried out in unspeakable terror:

–Mother, get me out of here!

That implacable tide that rose slowly, without stopping, already covered him up to his neck, and suddenly, as if the weight that gravitated over him had suffered a sudden increase, a new detachment took place and the livid head with its hair bristling with fright disappeared, his hoarse cry of agony extinguished instantaneously. But a moment later it appeared again, the eyes out of the orbits and the open mouth full of sand.

The mother, furiously digging the quicksand, had once again managed to uncover the bruised face of her son, and a terrible struggle then ensued around the blonde head of the dying man. The old woman, on her knees, with the help of her hands, her arms and her body, rejected the sandy waves that were rising when the last sinking took place. The solid bark eaten underneath broke in several places. Those near the edges felt the floor suddenly giving way beneath their feet and rolled in confused pile into the hole. The well had become blinded, the sand covered the woman up to her shoulders and rose more than a meter above Valentín's head.

When, after an hour of hard work, the body was removed, the sun had already finished its run, the plain was filled with shadows, and from the west an immense beam of red, violet, and orange rays rose below the horizon and fanned out towards the zenith.

Juan Fariña

On the small promontory that penetrates into the blue waters of the gulf, still today can be seen the old constructions of the mine of... High chimneys of lime and brick are raised on the ruined storehouses that sheltered the machinery, whose pieces gnawed by urine rest immobile on their stone bases. The plungers no longer move forward or backward within the cylinders, and the enormous steering wheel stopped in its course looks like the wheel of a vehicle stuck in that overcrowding of debris eaten away by time.

At the top, dominating the liquid immensity, the black lines of some intersecting beams, stand out as a sinister and mysterious figure against the blue background of the sky. On the bitter slopes, the workers' houses show their sunken ceilings, and through the holes in the doors and windows, torn from their hinges, whitewashed walls filled with cracks can be seen in the deserted rooms. A few years ago this solitary spot was the seat of a powerful carboniferous establishment and life and movement animated those ruins where today no other rumor is heard than that of the waves, whipping the flanks of the mountain.

Dense columns of smoke escaped then from the enormous chimneys, and the rhythmic noise of the machines, together with the ascent and descent of the elevators in the pique, was never interrupted. Meanwhile, down there, in the staggered rooms at the foot of the hill, the voices of the women and the cheerful cries of the children were confused with the noise of the sea in that ever restless and turbulent place.

On a January morning, as the machine threw its gasping death rattle and the white scrolls of the steam faded into the warm air, becoming the finest rain, a man climbed up the road towards the mine. He was tall and by his clothes, covered by the red dust of the road, he looked more like a peasant than a worker. A sack tied with a strap hung from his back and his right hand held a thick stick, with which he probed the ground in front of him.

Very soon the stranger found himself on the platform of the mine, where he asked to be taken to the foreman's presence. The foreman, who was on his way to the mine down pit at that moment, stopped in surprise at the blind visitor.

–Friend –he said-, I'm the one you're looking for, who are you and what do you want?

–My name is Juan Fariña, and I want to work in the mine.

Those present looked at each other and smiled.

–And what do you want to take care of? –the foreman continued in a somewhat mocking tone.

–I want to work a hewer –answered quietly the blind man.

A murmur started from the group of workers surrounding the edge of the entrance of the mine and some compressed laughter exploded.

–Comrade –said the foreman, contemplating the strong musculature of the postulant-, no doubt you won't need the strength, but to be a hewer you have to have a good eye and a blind man like you won't do the job.

–I don't see anything –he replied-, but I have good hands and I'm not afraid of any work.

–You are accepted –said the foreman, after a moment of hesitation-, a blind man who does not ask for alms and wishes to work deserves to be welcomed; you can start when you like.

–Tomorrow, first thing in the morning, I will be here –replied the original character, and he walked away, passing with his head upright and his white pupils fixed in the void between the mob of workers admiring his wide shoulders and his muscular athlete's body.

In the morning of the following day, Juan Fariña, with the miner's blouse and trousers, a small basket with a snack in one hand and a cane in the other, entered the cage accompanied by a foreman and several workers. All covered their heads with the traditional leather cap and in all of them, except the blind man's, attached to the visor, a small oil lamps shone. At a signal from the chief, the cage suddenly sank into the black abyss from which a light mist rose, condensing into crystalline droplets along the flexible steel cables.

When the descent was over, they went into the mine, following the dark corridors along which the blind man, who walked with the ease of an experienced miner. His companions admired that kind of instinct that made him guess the obstacles and avoid them with astonishing sagacity. His staff was an antenna that moved nimbly in all directions, touching the walls, the floor and the roof of the galleries, which as he advanced, inclined more and more, forcing him to bend his tall stature and to touch with his back the rough rock.

Soon they left the drag galleries and penetrated the quarries from where the material is extracted. In some places they crawled on their hands and knees, they went into those narrow tunnels, going up and down along very steep slopes. Everywhere there was an incessant beating: the dull noise of the picks biting the lode, mixed with the clearest sound of the hammers on the lode. Sometimes a violent impregnation ripped through that unbreathable environment, impregnated with smoke and coal dust; deep groans and a continuous puffing of fatigued beasts came out of those holes in the middle of the darkness, in which the fugitive lights of the lamps appeared and disappeared like fatuous fires in the shadows of the night.

After half an hour of painful march they stopped at a small open excavation in the vein. Rectangular in shape, very low and narrow, it was barely a meter high, and on its black walls, wounded by the deadly rays of the lamps, the sharp edges of the coal took on blue and bright dyes. After listening quietly to the foreman's directions, the new worker resolutely penetrated the narrow opening, and very soon his fatigued breathing and the repeated dry blow of steel were confused with the dull rumbling that filled the galleries, the draughts of air, and the dreary revolts.

From that day on, Fariña was incorporated into the personnel of the mine, and he later earned a reputation as an intelligent and courageous worker. The deference with which he was treated by the chiefs and his sullen and withdrawn character alienated him from the sympathies of his comrades, who could not understand that the blind man preferred the works and miseries of the miner to the free life, without worries, of the beggar. That was unnatural and had to involve some mystery. Intrigued they watched him closely, scrutinizing his steps and his minor actions. His past was the object of a meticulous investigation, which did not yield any results. No one knew who he was or where he came from, and with regard to his blindness opinions were divided. There were those who asserted that those still pupils covered with a whitish matter, threw phosphorescent flashes like those of the cat into the darkness, and that the blind man was only blind in broad daylight, under the light of the sun. Others, and they were very few, maintained the opposite, and to clarify the point they subjected the unhappy one to the most barbaric tests. It was already a wagon overturned in the middle of the road, which intercepted his step, or a wood crossed at the height of his head, against which he crashed violently; while invisible wires entangled between his legs knocked him down in the black and viscous mud of the galleries.

Time passed, and the unknown worker enthused more and more the tempers inside the mine. Strange rumors began to circulate about his work in the quarries. Every day at sunrise he was by the mine entrance ready to go down and he was always one of the last ones to take the elevator to return to his lonely room at the foot of the hill. During those fifteen hours of hard work, a number of wagons greater than the minimum number required would be pulled from the reef. This disconcerted the hardest hewers, because in that place the ore was hard and consistent and the best of them had never achieved such a success.

This fact strengthened in the credulous imagination of those simple people the belief that Fariña was an extraordinary being. It was told of him that he was only going to the mine to sleep and that a partner whose name they did not dare to pronounce, released from the vein the coal necessary to complete the task of the day. And it was no mystery to anyone that at night, when the mine was deserted, a furious roll -that did not cease until dawn- was heard in the cursed quarry. That indefatigable worker, who was spoken of quietly and fearfully, was but the Devil, who wandered day and night in the depths of the mine, giving mysterious blows in the abandoned quarries, making the rocks fall off and opening way through invisible cracks to the traitorous exhalations of the firedamp.

Two old miners in charge of guarding the ventilation corridors at night had cautiously approached the place from where the unusual rumor started, stopping in awe at the presence of an unknown hewer at the bottom of the blind man's quarry, furiously attacking the black and brittle block. A jet of burning firedamp gushed from a crack in the ceiling spreading a clear light around the fantastic character, in front of whom the coal threw strange reflections and its whimsical facets shone like polished jet before the blue flame of the fearsome gas.

Witnesses to that scene saw coal piling up with astonishing speed in front of the unknown nocturnal worker, when suddenly a piece torn off with force from the ignoble block knocked down two pieces of wood cladding resting on the wall, which, falling on top of each other, formed by a strange chance a cross on the humid floor of the corridor.

A terrible explosion thundered the vault and a gust of air whipped the faces of the two workers, nailed to the site by the terror, until the infernal vision suddenly disappeared.

The next morning both were found fainted at the bottom of a badly ventilated gallery, and from that moment no one doubted in the mine that a dark pact linked the abhorred blind man with an evil spirit. To the antipathy professed by the miners was then added a superstitious fear, and as they went by they rushed away, devoutly pursuing each other. His neighbors in the quarry left their work and moved to another place, and the truck driver in charge of dragging the wagons refused to do that work, forcing Fariña to be both hewer and wheelbarrow operator at the same time.

Whether because of that excess of work, whose overwhelming fatigue would have broken the most robust constitution, or because of another unknown cause, his taciturnity increased from day to day and his muscular body gradually lost that aspect of strength and vigor that contrasted so nobly with the weak context of the miners, those outcasts of the air and the light that carried printed on their wax faces the nostalgia of the fields illuminated by the sun.

A visible decay was taking place in him, and the workers who observed him attributed it to the fact that the end of the nefarious covenant must be near and it was an undisputed truth that an extraordinary event of which they might soon be witnesses, was being prepared inside the mine, giving more strength to those suppositions the increasingly strange conduct of the blind man. He was frequently seen to leave the quarry and penetrate the seldom frequented galleries, leaving at night his solitary dwelling to wander like a ghost by the seashore, and sometimes sitting on the stones of the shore he spent hours after hours, hearing the eternal murmur of the waves, like an old wolf resting from his runs across the ocean.

What did he think in those moments and what hidden pain kept his soul closed to all affection? About the origin of his blindness, no one ever knew anything.

Soon he was going to complete one year in the mine, but the mystery of his life remained impenetrable. Among the various rumors that circulated about him was one that was forgotten for everybody. The oldest miners vaguely remembered that many years ago, victim of one of the frequent explosions of firedamp, a worker perished in the mine, and his sixteen-year-old son who accompanied him was left badly wounded. As a result of that misfortune the wife of the unhappy worker and mother of the child lost her mind, and the fate of the boy was completely ignored. Those who remembered those facts believed to see in Fariña's face vestiges of ancient burns; but things did not pass from there and the mystery always subsisted.

The miners saw in that blind man an enemy of their tranquility and of the existence of the mine itself. No good could be expected of a man who had a covenant with the Devil, and the alarmists announced all sorts of evils for the future, citing him to support those sinister omens, some enigmatic words spoken after a collapse that had taken the lives of several workers.

–When I die, the mine will die with me –said the mysterious blind man.

For many that phrase contained a threat and for others a prophecy that would soon be fulfilled.

In the week that preceded the great catastrophe, Fariña obtained the position of night watchman of that section of the mine where he worked, a job whose performance was relatively easy, since the main task consisted in going through the ventilation gates. On the night of the extraordinary event, he presented himself as usual at the entrance of the mine at the regular time: at nine o'clock he marked the clock of the machine when he entered the cage and disappeared into the down pit.

It was a holiday and the mine was deserted. The weather was tempestuous, thick clouds covered the sky and the north wind, blowing violently at the top of the hoist, made the wood moan, shaking the cables along the levels. The sea was rough and tumultuous and the tide raised its hoarse voice between the reefs of the coast.

The engineer, with one hand on the regulator and the other on the brake, closely followed the indicator hand. The machine worked at high speed, as the task was reduced to drawing water from the pit by means of large buckets suspended beneath the lifting cages. And next to the edge of the entrance of the mine a worker armed with a long iron hook opened the floodgates placed at the bottom of those, which gave way to the water that drained through the drainage channel. These two men and the stoker, who was roasting in the boiler department, were the only ones watching the mine at that time.

Meanwhile, Fariña had left the elevator and walked through the central gallery, dodging the obstacles with the peculiar ease that he had.

In front of the door of the foremen's department he stopped, and by jumping the lock he penetrated into the interior; he took from a closet near to the wall a number of small, cylindrical packages which he buried in the pockets of his blouse and immediately seized a bag of gunpowder and some rolls of fuses, left the room and went deep into the mine. He marched hastily, sliding quietly between the rows of empty wagons, and soon set aside the main arteries to enter an abandoned gallery, which served only as a ventilation corridor.

This site had always been the subject of special surveillance by the engineers. Located under the sea, the leaks were abundant in that gallery and the threat of sinking was an idea that had worried the bosses and operators for many years. The mysterious rumors of the ocean reached that place through the thin layer of land that separated the sea from the tunnels, and the noise of the blades of the propellers hitting the waves was distinctly perceived, because the gallery cut obliquely the route of the vapors that touched the port. Considerable cladding work had been carried out to prevent the bottom of the sea from giving way under the pressure of the waters. In the place where the seepage was most copious, thick beams resting on solid pilasters supported the roof. Next to one of these supports Fariña stopped, extracting behind him a moldy carpenter's drill.

Six of those pillars were perforated at the height of one meter. With the help of the drill, he removed the clay that hid the holes, and with the calm and certainty that indicated he was carrying out a long meditated operation, he introduced in each of them a cartridge of dynamite with its corresponding fuse, forming with those long strands, all of the same length, a single bunch, whose extremities he carefully equalized; and tying them immediately with a twine, he poured over the thick knot a part of the gunpowder sack, tracing with the rest a trickle on the floor, some meters long. The main task was finished, and the author of that unnoticed and terrible work stood up and, extending his arm, struck the damp roof with the ferrous tip of his staff as if he wanted to calculate the thickness of the rock on which the moving mass of the ocean gravitated.

After a moment he bowed again: in his right hand a lighted match glowed and a stream of sparks swiftly traversed the ground, suddenly becoming an intense flame that illuminated the innermost parts of the gallery. The sinister character then retreated about twenty meters along the path he had traversed, standing motionless with his arms crossed in the middle of the corridor. In front of him a slight sputtering barely interrupted that silence of death, when suddenly a dry boom rumbled like thunder and one of the pillars cut in two flew in splinters under the black vault. Seconds later a terrible explosion violently pushed the air and a huge pile of shattered woods intercepted the gallery. For a few moments the rock cracked, followed by abrupt detachments, first small chunks bounced dully off the fallen masonry, then, like the stopper of an empty bottle submerged in deep water, the roof of the tunnel gave way with a single stroke, limpid flashes of lightning snaked for a moment in the dark, and something like the gallop of heavy squadrons resounded with a frightening thunder in the mine.

Outside, the unleashed tempest bellowed with fury, and the wind and the sea confused their irritated voices into a single sound, sharp and loud. The engineer, standing on the platform of the machine, fixed a drowsy gaze on the indicator and the rim of the well, next to which the iron hook worker performed his task shivering with cold under his damp clothes. They had both thought they could hear strange rumors among the noise of the squall that seemed to come from below, from the bottom of the mine down pit, believing that sometimes they saw that the cables lost their tension as if the weight they bore was diminished by some unknown cause.

During those long hours the two men stared at the bucket and looked up anxiously with the vain hope of seeing the liquid stream diminish or cease altogether. How unaware they were that the water which ran down the slope of the mountain and mixed with that of the sea did but return to its reservoir of origin! By dawn the force of the storm diminished, and the workman by the pit suddenly felt in the drainage channel strong blows, as if something living were stirring in it. He approached the place from which that extraordinary noise had begun, and was perplexed, dumb with astonishment, at the sight of an object which seemed to throw lightning, and which was violently whipping by the grate of the canal. He quickly took a lamp hanging from one of the goat's beams, and his surprise turned to fright: what was jumping in there was a living fish, a silver-bellied sea bass. Meanwhile the engineer became impatient waiting for the prescribed signals, and his imperative calls dominated the noise of the wind, which grew louder and louder as the day progressed.

At last the reluctant worker reappeared on the platform, holding the fish, which was violently contracting its viscous body, suspended by its tail. The man in the machine, seeing the object moving in his companion's hand, shouted from on high:

–What's the matter, Juan, what's the matter?

–Nothing, we are draining the sea –it was the brief answer that wounded his ears.

After a few minutes, the alarm whistle sounded in the mine for the last time, shocking its dormant inhabitants, and the steam, the vital breath of that iron organism, left the cylinders and boilers forever, escaping through the open valves in the midst of chilling whistles.

The workers came and gathered in consternation around the entrance of the mine, contemplating silently the engineers who, by means of probes, verified the disaster. From time to time, subterranean clicks produced by the collapses of the interior works resounded dully. The sea water filled the whole mine and went up the well until it was fifty metres from the edges of the excavation.

Fariña's name was on all lips, and no one doubted for a moment that he was the author of the catastrophe that freed them forever from that prison where so many generations had languished in the midst of torture and unknown miseries.

* * *

Every year, on the night of the anniversary of the terrible accident that destroyed one of the most powerful coalfields in the region, the fishermen on these shores report that near the steep promontory, on the route of the ships that touch the port, when the first stroke of twelve o'clock in the night sounds in the tower of the distant church, a small, boiling, foamy whirlpool is formed in the salty waves, and the formidable figure of the blind man with his pupils fixed in the desolate, dead mine emerges from that funnel

Along with the last vibration of the bell, the fearful apparition fades away, and a foam stain marks the dangerous place, from which the fishing boats quickly flee, driven by their agile rowers, and woe to those who venture too close to that miniature Maelstrom, because attracted by a mysterious force and roughly shaken by the waves, they will be at imminent risk of capsizing.

Big Game Hunting

In the dilated and arid plain, the rays of the sun bask the grass that grows among the bushes, whose stunted shrubs intertwine their weak and crawling branches with the twisted spirals of the parasitic plants of dry and dusty leaves.

In the bare paths the black and thick sand burns, and among the bushes you can hear the noise produced by the snakes and lizards that, fed up with light and heat, slide looking for a little shade between the brief branching of the myrtle and the stems of the thistles erect and dry.

With the body bent and the rifle between his trembling hands, the Pigeon, a small old man as dry as a hazelnut, with short steps on his hesitant legs, follows the traces left by the partridges' footprints in the calcined sand of the paths.

No one like him could distinguish between a thousand fresh and recent footprints and know whether the bird is a male or female, a chicken or an adult. Alone, with no relatives to protect him in his helpless old age, he satisfies his most pressing needs with the product of the hunt.

The rays of the sun, falling plumb on his hunched back, made his march on that soft and shifting ground more painful. His fatigue was great, and he had not yet fired a shot when he suddenly rose to his feet, stopping before a group of hawthorns and stunted litre trees: the trail so patiently followed ended there. He circled the bush, watching the ground carefully to make sure that the bird had not slipped out the other way, and lifting the trigger he peered between the branches, stretching his neck and steepening at the tip of his feet.

The three fingers marked in the sand, projected forward like a fan indicated a superb male.

His restless, vivacious eyes that recorded every leaf, every stalk of grass, soon discovered the yellow beak and dark head poking out of the bifurcation of a branch. The body, the color of the dry leaf, was rather guessed, since it was hidden within the foliage. A magnificent partridge with feathers half-scorched by the flash took its place in the empty backpack.

Cheerful and satisfied, he immediately set out to load the rifle, whose moldy barrel of excessive length and gauge was attached to the box by ties of string and twine. A piece of wood fixed in a hole at the end of the old instrument was used as a sight, a piece that had to be renewed after each shot, because it was carried in front of the piece of the interior that served as its base and very often the effectiveness of the shot was due to this improvised projectile more deadly than a simple pellet. With the use the hole had been enlarged and the thickness of the sight increased in proportion. When aiming, the view was intercepted by a monolith behind which an elephant would not be seen.

The solemn gravity with which he handled the weapon demonstrated the importance given to this operation. Once the gunpowder bottle was uncovered, he poured the black and lustrous powder into the palm of his hand and, approaching the mouth of the barrel, he emptied it slowly, carefully blowing the grains adhered to his dry and rough skin. He calmly pushed the bunch of grass that served as a taco, and then in the hollow of his hand he meticulously counted the Twelve Peers, twelve round and shiny pellets by rubbing them between his fingers like precious objects, and two by two –to establish the count– he dropped them into the enormous barrel. Finally, taking a pellet thicker than the others, before releasing it, he traced with it the sign of the cross in the mouth of the cannon: it was Charlemagne who was going to keep company to his knights.

Once the task was finished, blinded by the dazzling clarity that radiated from above, with one hand in front of his eyes as a screen, he explored the horizon, undecided about the direction he should follow, when the whistle of the partridge that takes flight and twitches the nerves of the most phlegmatic made him turn quickly. To his right, in a slight depression of the ground, he perceived distinctly the bird falling with rapid flutter. In a few minutes he saved the distance and approached cautiously, with infinite precautions, following the track engraved in the sand he discovered the piece crouched between the thistles. He rested the butt on his shoulder and released the shot. The smoke of the shot still did not dissipate in the scorched atmosphere when a reddish lump passed by like a tornado and grazed his hesitating legs, making him stumble.

He cried out in surprise and anger:

–Get off, Napoleon!

But it was too late: the partridge whose neck had been pierced by the sight had just disappeared into the jaws of an enormous tawny-colored hunting dog.

Passed the first moment of stupor, with the rifle in high he rushes on the intruder and full of courage tries to hit the thief with it, blows that the dog avoids with great facility, giving sudden jumps between the bushes without releasing his prey. Fatigued and panting, he stopped leaning on the barrel of his old carbine. Anger had been followed by the painful anguish experienced in the face of an irreparable loss. Such a beautiful piece, a prince's delicacy, swallowed up by that filthy little animal. His eyes moistened, and changing tactics, with a trembling voice that he tried to make affectionate, he repeated:

–Napoleon, good dog, come here, little son.

Meanwhile the good dog sniffed the ground, picking up the crumbs of the feast, and when the banquet was over, the feathered muzzle appeared among the leaves, licking itself greedily, and fixing on the stunned hunter his eyes shining like embers, he seemed very willing to correspond to his manifestations of affection. With a jump he came out of the thickness and with a joyful air, wagging with vivacity the diminutive tail, he went to rub his muzzle to detach the feathers in the not very solid legs of the old man.

Faced with the cynicism and shamelessness of that evil creature, he felt that courage returned to him and for an instant only ideas of blood and extermination sprouted from his enraged brain. They gave him the impetus to empty the gunpowder bottle and the whole bag of pellets into the weapon and then to unlock that atrocious shot on the infamous bandit, throwing it into the air.

Soon he appeased himself: the master of the dog was the butler of the hacienda, an authoritarian and brutal man who would have cruelly avenged any offense made to his favorite.

The bull mastiff's fondness for partridges was recent and dated back to the day when one of these birds, wounded in flight by an accurate shot, fell between his legs. The mouthful must have tasted glorious, because from then, hear a shotgun and rush off, was all one.

That day, attracted by the first shot the dog had arrived in time to take advantage of the second one.

The old man, disheartened and sad, without thinking about revenge, was moving away with a tardy step from that unhappy place when he soon stopped surprised. His backpack had tripled in weight. He glanced over his shoulder and his grey eyes flashed. The bull mastiff, holding the sack with his teeth, tried to detach it from the cord that held it. Jesus Christ! What wrath he took upon him: he straightened his small size and, taking the rifle by the barrel, he briskly shot the damned beast through the butt, but he only wounded the air, his weak legs incapable of resisting the impulse of the heavy weapon bent and he fell how long it was in the undergrowth, cruelly scratching his hands and face.

For a long time he huddled on the ground with the weapon between his legs, as he thought how to get rid of the intruder who, sitting in his hindquarters, two steps away, looked at him shamelessly, with a look between surprised and annoyed at the delay in continuing the interrupted hunt. Opening his wide mouth, he yawned with deaf grunts of impatience, and believing that the hunter's attitude was due to a momentary forgetfulness, he wanted to remind him of his duties by example.

Like a retriever dog, quickly wagging his short, thick tail, his snout stuck to the ground, snorting noisily, he went through the undergrowth, raising clouds of tanagers and chincoles[1], putting to flight the lizards that slept between the leaves. From time to time he stopped; he lifted his head, glancing at the immobile old man, and began the task again with greater vigor.

Finally the old man got up and, as if the hunt was over, he put his rifle on his shoulder and began to walk with indifferent attitude through the most arid and exposed places. But the stratagem had no effect. The dog followed him with his head lowered, reluctantly, but without moving away from his heels. Exasperated by that stubborn persecution he had a last resort: he dropped his weapon on one side of the path and with his hands in his pockets, like an unemployed man walking to stretch his legs, he continued walking without turning his head. The trick was a decisive success: after a short stretch, Napoleon, throwing him a glance sideways, took the lead, away at the trot with the tail down and ears down, without looking back.

At last he was free, and rubbing his eyes, as if waking from a nightmare, he saw the damned animal disappear jubilantly. It was still time to recover what had been lost, and striving to overcome tiredness and fatigue, he recovered his rifle and went into a grove of boldos[2] and myrtles. The partridges harassed on the plain by the heat must have sought refuge in the thicket. He was not deceived; numerous traces were seen everywhere. He set to work with eagerness, scrutinizing the decaying trunks and scanning the dark corners under the emerald green leaves of the vóquiles without being distracted by the noise of broken branches that he thought he heard every moment in the undergrowth. No doubt he would be some fox interrupted in his nap that left the lair with his restless and cautious step.

His perseverance was soon rewarded: a partridge recklessly advancing its head, spied on him from behind a log. He extended his arm and pressed the trigger. After the boom, the branches moved away violently and the head of the dog appeared with his ears stiff and straight. He jumped over the partridge and began to crush it between its powerful jaws. The weapon escaped from the hands of the old man. The astonishment, the anger, the pain and the deepest discouragement were painted on his face. He felt defeated, without the strength to fight, and a deep sorrow overwhelmed his troubled spirit. What could he do, a decrepit old man, thrown from everywhere like a useless bundle, against that fierce and formidable enemy capable of strangling him with a single bite!

He resignedly picked up the rifle and, as he emptied his last load of gunpowder, two thick tears slipped down his spindly cheeks and, passing through his grey whiskers, humidified his lips: they were bitter as gall.

Everything around him was wild and untamed. Murky vapors rose from the side of the sea over the resting dunes. Not a grain of sand slipped on its brown slopes, that the stillness of the air stopped in its endless advance on the limitless plain. The space flooded with light contrasted with

---

1 *Zonotrichia capensis.*
2 *Peumus boldus.*

the slate soil of languid and scarce vegetation from which a breath of fire was exhaled. Overwhelmed by the heat, he climbed painfully up the steep slope to reach the road, when a sudden pull made him turn around on himself and losing his balance, he came to earth with a roar. He rose halfway up: Napoleon descended gallantly down the slope, carrying the backpack hanging from his mouth. A flare erupted from the old man's extinguished eyes, and blood in boiling waves swirled to his heart and brain, giving him back for an instant the vigor of youth. Never had his pulse been so firm, nor his eye so sure...! A resounding howl answered the detonation: the bull mastiff released the backpack and with his back hairs bristling like spikes disappeared into the bushes. After the first outburst of anger, the old man felt that his blood was freezing in his veins and a deep numbness seized his whole being. His servant's soul experienced a supreme faintness. He believed he had committed an enormous crime, and the figure of the enraged master appeared to his imagination, giving him a shiver of terror. He looked at the plain, and he saw there the dog crossing the sandbanks: he was in a hell of a hurry: embedded in the base of his tail he carried Charlemagne and scattered on his back under his hirsute skin, the Twelve Pairs. Like the roe deer which senses he is pursued by the hounds, the old man rose with vigorous impulse and bent as never before, dragging its heavy feet, disappeared after a bend in the dusty road.

The Search

The morning is cold, hazy, a fine drizzle drenches the stunted scrub of old boldos[1] and stunted litre trees. The grandmother, with her rolled up skirt and bare feet, hurries along the narrow path, avoiding as much as possible the rubbing of the branches, from which thick droplets drip off and pierce the soft and spongy soil of the shortcut. That path is a rarely used, a solitary trail that, deviating from the black road, leads to a small population distant about five miles from the powerful coal establishment, whose constructions appear from time to time between the clearings of the forest there in the blurred distance of the horizon.

Despite the cold and the rain, the old lady's face is soaked in sweat and her breath is choppy and gasping. On her right hand, leaning against her chest, she carries a package whose volume she tries to hide among the folds of her worn woolen shawl.

The grandmother is short, thin and dry. Her face, full of wrinkles with dark and sad eyes, has a humble, resigned expression. She seems very restless and suspicious, and as the trees diminish, her fear and fright become more visible.

When she reaches the edge of the forest, she pauses for a moment to look closely at the open space that stretches out in front of her like an immense grey sheet, under the slate sky, almost black in the direction of the northeast.

---

1 *Peumus boldus.*

The sandy, barren plain was deserted. To the right, interrupting their monotonous uniformity, the white walls of the sheds were crowned by the smooth zinc roofs glistening from the rain. And beyond, almost touching the heavy clouds, the black plume of smoke, twisted, crumbled by the furious gusts of the north, emerged from the enormous chimney of the mine. The old woman, always fearful and restless, after an instant of observation, passed her thin body through the wires of the fence that bordered on that side the grounds of the establishment, and headed straight for the rooms. From time to time she would bend over and pick up the wet brushwood, splinters, branches, dry roots scattered in the sand, with which she formed a small bundle which, tied with a string, was placed on his head.

With this trophy she made his way into the corridors, but the ironic glances, the smiles and the double entendre words that addressed her as she passed by, made her see that the ruse was too familiar and did not deceive the perceptive eyes of her neighbors.

But, sure of the reserve of those good people, she did not give importance to their jokes and did not stop until she found herself in front of the door of her house. She put the key in the lock, turned the door on its hinges, and once inside she bolted the door.

After throwing the firewood bundle into a corner and carefully placing the package on top of the bed, she stripped herself of the shawl and suspended it from a string that ran through the room at the height of her head.

Then she lit the pile of shavings and charcoal that was ready in the chimney and sat in front on a small bench, waiting.

A bright flame rose from the stove and illuminated the room on whose white bare and cold walls the angular and fantastic shadow of the grandmother was drawn.

When the heat was enough, she put the teapot with water for the mate on the irons and going to bed she unwrapped the package and placed its contents, one pound of yerba mate[2] and one pound of sugar, at one end of the bench where the chipped earthenware well and the tin drinking straw were already lying.

As the fire sizzles, the old woman caresses with her dry fingers the fine, lustrous yerba of a beautiful green color, delighting herself beforehand with the exquisite drink that her gourmand's mouth is eager to savor.

Yes, the desire to taste a mate from that aromatic and fragrant grass had long been an obsession in her, a fixed idea of her sexagenarian brain. But how difficult it had been until then for her to obtain the satisfaction of that appetite, her vice, as she said; for her granddaughter José, the porter of the mine, earned so little, barely thirty cents a day, which was indispensable not to starve to death. And the boy was the only breadwinner in her family of two people!

While the yerba mate in the company store was so mediocre and had such bad taste, there in the village there was a very fine, pure leaf and so aromatic that just remembering it would make his mouth water. But it was

---

2 Y*erba mate* is an infusion that is usually taken alone and occasionally accompanied with medicinal or aromatic herbs.

so expensive, forty cents a pound! It is true that she paid double at the company store, but the payment was made with tokens or vouchers on account of the child's salary, while to acquire the other one was necessary hard cash.

But that was not the only difficulty. There was also a strict prohibition for all the workers of the mine to buy anything, neither provisions, nor a pin, nor a piece of cloth outside the Company's office. Any article of other origin was declared contraband and confiscated on the spot, and recidivism was punished with the immediate expulsion of the smuggler.

For long months she treasured penny after penny in a corner of the bed, under the mattress, the amount she needed. Taking care that her grandson had what was necessary, she deprived herself of what was indispensable and, little by little, the pile of copper coins increased until finally the sum collected was not only enough to buy a pound of yerba mate, but also a bit of sugar, the kind of white and crystalline sugar that was never seen in the company store.

But now came the difficult part. To go to the village, make the purchase and then return without arousing the suspicions of the guards, who like an Argos with a hundred eyes watched the comings and goings of the people. She was frightened and lost her determination. What would become of her and of the child in that winter that appeared so crude if they threw them out of the room, leaving her without bread or a roof over her head?

But the money was there, tempting her, as if telling her:

–Come on, take me, don't be afraid.

She chose a rainy day when the surveillance was going to be relaxed and, very early, as soon as the little one had left for the mine, she took the coins, locked the door, and went into the plain, carrying the roll of ropes that she used to tie the bundles of firewood that she was going to collect from time to time in the woods.

But once she was far enough away, she crossed the wire-fence and took the narrow path which, avoiding the long detour of the road, led in a straight line towards the village.

The distance was long, very long for her poor and weak legs, but she traveled it without great fatigue thanks to the mild temperature and the nervous excitement that possessed her.

It was not so easy on the way back. The road seemed rough, endless, and she had to stop at times to catch her breath. Then, she experienced a great anxiety for the accomplishment of that crime to which her guilty conscience gave disturbing proportions.

The mockery of the dreaded ban on shopping outside the company store was as overwhelming as the consummation of a monstrous robbery. And at every moment she seemed to see behind every tree the threatening silhouette of a guard who suddenly threw himself on her and pulled out the proof of her crime.

Several times she was tempted to throw the compromising package to one side of the road to get rid of that anguish, but the aromatic fragrance of the herb that through the wrapper caressed her sense of smell made her desist from practicing such a painful action.

That is why when she found herself safe inside her room, free of any indiscreet gaze, she was attacked by a childish access of joy.

And while the water ready to boil let escape the joyful run run that precedes the boiling, the grandmother, with her hands crossed in her lap, followed with the sight the tenuous wisps of steam that began to escape by the curved beak of the teapot.

In spite of the atrocious tiredness caused by the very long walk, she experienced a sweet sensation of happiness. She was finally going to taste again the exquisite mates of yesteryear, the same ones that were her delight until they were taken away from her by that insatiable devourer of youth: the mine, that under its plants, in the depth of the earth extended the black net of its passages, hell and ossuary of so many generations.

Suddenly, a hard knock on the door ripped her from her meditations. A terrible fear took hold of her and mechanically, almost unaware of what she was doing, she took the package and hid it under the bench. A second blow more severe than the first one was followed by a rough and imperious voice that shouted: Open, grandmother, soon, soon! pulled her out of her immobility. She got up and unlocked the bolt.

The head of the office and his young clerk were the first ones to cross the threshold, followed by two guards carrying large sacks on their backs, which they deposited on the bricked floor. The old woman had fallen on the bench.

Immobile, paralyzed, she looked in front of her with the face of an idiot; and her half-opened mouth and the fallen jaw revealed the height of surprise and fright. The imposing figure of that gentleman with the blonde beard and twisted whiskers, wrapped in his luxurious coat, took colossal proportions, filled the room, preventing any attempt to slip away and hide.

Meanwhile, the clerk, a sharp and agile young man, aided by the guards, had begun the search. After throwing aside the bed covers, turning the mattress and feeling the straw over the cloth, they opened the small trunk and, one by one, they threw into the center of the room the rags it contained, making equivocal comments about those garments, so broken and frayed, that there was nowhere to pick them up. Then they rummaged through the corners, removed the scarce and miserable utensils from their places, and suddenly stopped looking at each other's face in disorientation.

The chief, standing in front of the door, in a severe and dignified attitude, watched the movements of his subordinates without detaching his lips.

The clerk, addressing one of the men, asked him:

–Are you sure you saw her go through the fences?

The questioned man replied:

–So sure, sir, as I'm seeing you now. She came out of the shortcut and would bet ten against one she came from the village.

There was a small silence that the chief's brief voice interrupted:

–Well, search her now.

While the two men took the old woman by the arms and held her upright, the young man carried out the odious operation in an instant.

–She has nothing –he said, wiping his wet hands as he walked through the folds of wet clothing.

And everything would have ended happily for the grandmother if the young man, in his eagerness not to leave any place without searching it fully, had not approached the bench and looked down it.

He had hardly bowed when he straightened up and directed his radiant gaze of joy towards his boss.

–See where she had it, sir, this old woman of the devil!

The master ordered dryly:

–Take that away and leave.

When the clerk and the guards had gone out, the chief contemplated for a moment the wretched and shabby figure of the old woman who had shrunk and curled up on the seat:

–If you weren't a poor old woman right now, I would make you vacate the room, throwing you into the street. And this, in conscience, would be fair, for you know very well, grandmother, that to buy something outside the office is a theft from the Company. For now and for the first time I forgive you, but for another time I will strictly do my duty. Stay with God and ask him to forgive you this sin so dishonorable to your gray hairs.

The grandmother was left alone. Her chest was overflowing with gratitude for the goodness of the master and she would have fallen on her knees at his feet, if surprise and fear had not paralyzed her. Without rising from her seat she turned to the chimney and bowed her head heavily.

Outside the bad weather increases by degrees; some bursts open the door and fan the dying fire, swirling on the nape of the old lady the grey and scarce hairs that expose her long and thin neck with the rough skin attached to the vertebrae.

The Drill

–Those were really good times –said the grandfather, addressing his youthful auditorium, which heard him with their mouths open. Gold condors[1] ran like water and these dirty papers of today were not even known by name. There were only two mines: Chambeque and Alberto, but the coal was so close to the pits that, from each of them, many hundreds of tons per day were extracted.

That's when the people of Playa Negra wanted to cut us off by running a gallery that went from the basement of Playa Blanco right to Santa María. They would cut off from us all the coal that was left to the north, under the sea. As soon as we heard the news, everyone went to the Heights of Lotilla to see the new works that our opponents had begun with great activity. They had already armed the hoist of the mine pit almost in the same shore where the wave bursts in the high tides. The rogues wanted to work as little as possible to close our way. In the meantime our bosses were not content with just looking. They were studying how to stop the blow, and they were running up and down with their faces so long that they were pitiful.

I had just arrived at the mine pit one morning, when Don Pedro, the chief foreman, called me to tell me:

–Sebastián, how many are the hewers in your squad?

–Twenty, sir –I replied.

–Take the twenty –he commanded me– ten of the best and go with them to the Heights of Lotilla. I'll be there in an hour.

---

1 Old Chilean currency.

I went downstairs and chose my men, and before the hour we were together with a cloud of laborers, carpenters and mechanics on the middle of the slope of the hill overlooking the sea.

While the workers dismantled and levelled the terrain and the carpenters sawed the huge beams, the mechanics make the engine ready to run. They all made a racket of a thousand demons. Hewers from Chambeque and Alberto arrived at every moment. There was the flower and cream of the whole mine. None of them was less than twenty years old or more than twenty-five.

Suddenly word spread that the chief engineer was going to speak to us. It still seems to me I see him perched on a pile of wood giving us that speech whose words I still have in my memory. After shaming the conduct of the people of Playa Negra, who without any reason and against all rights wanted to corner us against the hill to seize the underwater coal that we had been the first to discover and exploit, he told us that he counted with our drive and enthusiasm for the work to prevent that plundering that would be the ruin of all of us. Then he explained to us, albeit very briefly, what he demanded of us. In spite of his reserve and the vague nature of certain details, we understood that his intention was to open a hole in the place where we were and immediately a gallery parallel to the beach that would cross the line that come from Playa Negra. But for this plan to succeed, it was necessary to reach the crossroads before the opposites. And here was the difficult part, because the distance they had to cover was less than half the distance we had to cross to get to the same point under the sea.

At the end of the engineer's speech our enthusiasm was so great that we shouted out for the order to begin work immediately. We were furious against those of Playa Negra, and some proposed as the most practical thing to fix the problem to move on the intruders and to throw them inside their mine pit with hoist, machines and everything. The engineer appeased the exalted by telling them that violence would make the situation worse by postponing the difficulty indefinitely. It was best to fix this issue once and for all. After the men were calmed, the hewers were divided into twelve crews of ten men each, who would work one after the other, replacing each other every two hours. By this means there would always be at work people rested and refreshed.

We cast lots and my squad got the second turn. We waited impatiently for the changeover while the others with the highest numbers went home to sleep.

That was work! Naked, with a rag at our waist, we wielded with such rage the pickaxes that the earth, clay and stone seemed to us to be a soft thing in which we sank as a drill wick sinks into rotten wood. The sweat ran down our throats and we were steaming like the bar that the blacksmith removes from the forge and puts in the cooler. Some fainted, and when the foreman's whistle indicated that the shift was over, a fog darkened our sight and we could barely stand.

In the first week we reached sea level. Big pumps were put in to reduce the water and we continued digging and digging until the second week. Suddenly we were told to stop. The engineers came down with their instruments and after two hours or so they marked for us, with chalk, on the wall where we had to open the gallery. Without wasting a minute we took the tools and the work started with the same fury as before. We went down agile and fresh and two hours later we were unrecognizable, burst, almost dead. Outside the doctor took our pulse; we drank a little cognac with water and then went home to sleep. There were also some accidents. Suddenly one fell on his face and there he was without a leg. Others burst in blood through their noses and ears. Immediately were replaced by the reserve crew and the work went on day and night without stopping for a minute, even a second.

It was impossible to do more, but to the bosses it still seemed little. And it was no wonder, because we, who were going from south to north, to close the way to those of Playa Negra, who were going towards the east, had to travel a distance almost double. We had been working for a month, when one morning the engineers came to make a new measurement of the gallery. This time it took a long time. They talked, measured and measured again, and suddenly they ordered us to suspend the work until further notice. As we were dying of curiosity and wished to know if we had won or lost, no one wanted to leave the mine until they found out what was going on. I, as group leader, went to Don Pedro, the chief foreman, who was all the time with his ear attached to the wall and I asked him: –Did we make it yet?–. He gestured me to shut up, and then I put my ear to the wall. I listened for a while with all my soul and, suddenly, it seemed to me that I heard a few taps far away, as if someone were stroking the stone. I paid more attention, and when I was sure I was not mistaken, I called the foreman and said to him: –Don Pedro, this is where the drill is coming from.

He came and we listened together. Suddenly, by the light of the lamp, I saw how the foreman's eyes shone. The drilling blows were feeling stronger and stronger. At that moment the engineers arrived and after listening also with the ear stuck to the wall they unrolled a plane and began to work with their apparatuses. Then they marked with chalk a cross on the wall; they gave some orders to the foreman and they left, very happy. They had barely gone out when a dozen carpenters came down and hurriedly placed a door which closed a space of ten meters at the end of the gallery. The door was put in the frame and they caulked with great tidiness all cracks; finally the carpenters withdrew and only remained there the chief foreman and the work squad heads, hearing the blows given in the drill, which apparently was already very close. However, many hours passed and it was perhaps three o'clock in the afternoon when the foreman told me:

–Go upstairs and tell them to get the brazier ready.

I rushed to comply with the order, and when I was back the noise of the drill was so clear that I calculated that half an hour would not pass without the tip sticking out of the wall. The gallery was in that part two meters high and cut a layer of blue limestone that did not let seep a drop of water, though we had the sea above our heads. While we waited in silence, we never ceased to think of the engineers' calculations, whose accuracy filled us with admiration. We did not know, yet, that taking advantage of the little vigilance of the bosses of Playa Negra, two of ours had gone down to the opposite mine and wrote down their level and direction.

As I had already calculated, half an hour had not passed when the first pieces of limestone began to fall from the wall, a meter and a half from the ground. We all knew what this meant and waited with real eagerness for the guide drill to break through the wall to strike it with a hammer, making them realize that they had lost the game and that we were the masters under the sea. Maul in hand we waited for the right moment, when Don Pedro, the major foreman, signaled for us to move away; and affirming the left shoulder in the wall he spat on hid hands and waited with his eyes nailed to the limestone that rose like a blister.

I will never forget that moment. We all had our eyes fixed on the chief foreman, wanting to guess his intent. Lighted by the lamps, he looked like one of those giants that children's stories talk about. He was six feet tall and his thick body, enlarged by the glare of the lights, seemed to fill the narrow enclosure. His strength was famous throughout the mine. Many times I saw him joking, lifting a man in each hand and holding them in the air as if they were babies a few months old.

With one foot in front of the other, head a little inclined, he waited for the moment when the drill appeared through the wall. He did not have much time to wait. With each blow of the drill, the pieces of limestone that fell were larger, until, suddenly, something shiny came out of the wall, popping a thick slab. Quick as lightning, the foreman stroke it, and for a moment we felt his bones creaking. Suddenly he straightened up and stood still, leaning against the wall with his head thrown back and snorting like the bellows of a forge moved at full steam. We stared at the wall and could hardly believe what we saw. Bent into a square, the end of the drill protruded from the wall less than two feet and moved back and forth like the pendulum of a clock.

Grandfather paused, and after taking between his trembling fingers the lit cigarette that one of his attentive listeners offered him, he continued:

–What I have yet to tell you is very little. While the people of Playa Negra, who could not even remotely guess what had happened, blamed the incident on a simple blockage of their drill and made every imaginable effort to unblock it, widening the orifice, we had placed in front of it a large brazier of burning coal. Then the chief foreman ordered everyone to leave the gallery, the two of us staying there to finish the preparations. Everything was ready in a moment. After rehearsing whether the door closed well and while I was prudently going away, Don Pedro took in his arms, as if it were a feather, the enormous sack filled with chili pepper that had recently been lowered there, and, from the threshold, threw it over the burning embers. He closed the door with a kick, and turning back he ran towards the exit pit. I, who was ahead, was the first one to leave for the elevator, and although we were lifted immediately, we felt an itch in our throat when we reached the top, accompanied by an unbearable dry cough.

It wasn't ten minutes ago that we had left, when we saw that something extraordinary was happening in the enemy's mine. The alarm bell began to ring in a hurry, and something very serious must have been what was happening downstairs, because the ringing was desperate. As we were higher than they were, no detail escaped us. When the elevator appeared,

the mouth of the pit was full of people. Those who came out were surrounded and harassed by questions, which we heard perfectly:

–What's up, what's up?

But the poor devils could not answer, for a strange cough shook them
from head to toe. Then we all burst out shouting and cheering; the people of
Playa Negra answered with insults and blasphemies our cheers.

To finish, it only remains for me to say that all the attempts made
by our opponents to go down to the mine and resume work were useless.
Days, weeks and months passed and the impossibility was always the same.
As soon as the elevator sank in the pit a few meters, those who went in it
began to shout to be hoisted up without delay and came out half drowned,
coughing desperately.

It was impossible to have devised a more effective ploy. The smoke of
the chili pepper, enclosed in the master gallery, escaped so slowly through
the orifice of the drill-guide that it threatened never to be finished. And
what was meant to happen happened; that the roof of the gallery, shored up
lightly, collapsed, giving way to the sea water.

Six months later, the famous Playa Negra mine was just a well of
brackish water that the sand in the dunes was slowly filling up.

It was Him Alone...

That morning, while Gabriel, kneeling in front of the kitchen door, rubbed the white metal cutlery, he suddenly came up with the often cherished project of fleeing, of winning the mountain that surrounds the village to go immediately in search of his sisters. For some time now, the thought of meeting the little ones, of seeing them and talking to them, has been his constant concern. What good fortune have they had? Would they be happier than he? And he strove to believe it so, because the very idea that they should also have to suffer hardships like his, made him unspeakably distressed.

But, as always happened to him, the difficulties of the enterprise were presented to him with such characters that he became disheartened, conceptualizing it as unfeasible. The poor girls were so far away, and he lacked money and freedom to undertake the journey!

A deep despondency took hold of his spirit. He would be never able to overcome these obstacles! Suddenly, in one of those crises of despair that assailed him from time to time, he remained immobile for a few moments, with a gloomy face, his soul full of sadness.

Suddenly, the boisterous sounds of some music invaded the deserted street. It was band of street musicians, that crossed the town, inviting the neighbors to the function of the night. The music passed by and was escorted away by the town's children, whose voices and shouts stood out above the sharp notes of the clarinet.

On hearing that noise, it seemed to Gabriel that he was waking from a deep sleep. His pupils cheered up with a fleeting flame and his withered countenance became faintly colored. At one point he found himself transported to the not-too-distant times when he also ran after clowns; and the picture of his happy home, with his loving parents and graceful sisters, presenting in his memory vivid and tangible, evoked in his spirit a swarm of memories that pierced his heart like so many other daggers.

A dense fog tarnished his eyes, and pressing hard on his jaws to drown a groan soon to escape him, he lay face down on the hard ground. With his forehead resting on his crossed arms and his rigid body stretched out on the pavement, he made superhuman efforts to repress the sobs that, in uncontrollable waves, struggled to break the barrier opposed to them by the convulsed lips.

A quiet step resounded in the corridor, and almost at the same time, a female voice uttered choleric:

–Look, you've decided to burn my blood! It's lunchtime and the table isn't set yet! What are you doing lying here on the floor?

Gabriel, who had risen quickly, his countenance reddened, flooded with tears, turned towards the door and when he saw the threatening figure of the mistress, standing on the threshold, he hastily took the brush and the chalk, and with his eyes low he resumed the task in silence.

–I ask you, rascal, you don't you hear what I'm asking you? Why were you crying? Say, answer.

A vivid blush covered the little one's cheeks, and in a trembling voice he stammered softly and painfully, without looking up from the ground:

–I don't know, mistress; I was feeling sad.

–Ah, you were sad! and that's why the fire is almost extinguished and the cutlery is not completely clean. –And accentuating the mocking irony of her words, the lady continued: For that mischievous sorrow I am bringing here a holy, infallible remedy. In a Jesus, you will heal from sickness.

And saying and doing, she took out from under his apron a heavy whip and with the ease and the panache of an old practice, she raised it above her head.

But the sound of a knock on the street door stopped the right-handed flogger in the air. Hastily the mistress returned the whip to their place under the apron and left the kitchen, mumbling between her teeth with renewed anger:

–Wait, you'll pay for it!

* * *

In the small dining room, sitting at the head of the table, Mrs. Benigna, having on her right her neighbor and friend, Mrs. Encarnación Retamales and on her left her old uncle, a bachelor of sour and dismissive humor, does with kindness the honors of homeowner. His mellow voice has caressing inflections when she addresses Gabriel who comes and goes bringing the delicacies.

This simulation does not deceive the orphan, who knows too well that such softness will later be more than discounted by the implacable whip. With his arms rolled up and a white apron tied around his neck, he slides barefoot around the table.

The mistress, dressed in her invariable black merino suit, combed and groomed with care, shows herself cheerful and decisive, while Doña Encarnación, small and chubby, stuffed into a pompous dress of loud and vivid colors, barely speaks, very anxious with the unruly spring of her false teeth that persists in playing a trick on her. The old man, thick, corpulent, with a wide, puffy and purple face, eats sparingly, with great disgust from his niece, who reconvenes him with a mellifluous voice:

–Well, you're so despondent today, uncle; you barely taste what I serve you! Gabriel, little son, don't fall asleep, remove these plates.

Through the windows overlooking the courtyard, the midday light floods in, and in the room the atmosphere impregnated with the smell of food is warm, suffocating.

When lunch is over, and the old man had gone to take his usual nap, doña Benigna and her friend began their after lunch chat, exploiting, with wise erudition, the inexhaustible theme of provincial gossip.

When the little one, after raising the tablecloth, had left for the kitchen, doña Encarnación asks indifferently:

–What does this child have? He's so shrunken, so quiet. Is he sick, friend?

Doña Benigna replied lively:

–No, he's not sick. I reprimanded him, and since he has such a bad character, he still is sore. –And, suddenly changing his tone, she added, with a deep sigh:

–Ah, you can't imagine what this little boy makes me suffer! In the little time I have him at home, he has turn my hair grey...

–Heavy cross is to take care of other people's children. They also spoke to me to adopt one of this child's little sisters. Now I'm glad I didn't let them convince me, because what happened to you would have happened to me. These creatures have the arrogance of their family. Her father was an outrageous fellow. Poor thing! God keep him in his holy care; but I believe, and God forgive me, that he brought up his children very badly. They were the apple of his father's eye and he spoiled them; they say he never hit them. If I were you, I would take this child to the Orphans' House, because what obligation do you have to torment yourself with a person who is not of your blood?

–I promised to teach and educate him, and I am a slave to my word. To tell the truth, one have no worse enemy than one's good heart.

When pronouncing the last sentence, Doña Benigna felt that a knot oppressed her throat, and, suddenly experiencing the imperative need to be pitied and consoled, she painted with the blackest colors the picture of her life, cruelly bitter because of the conduct of the perverse creature that in a bad hour she welcomed into her home. She minutely recounted the setbacks that this monster of ingratitude provided her with his rebelliousness and arrogance in every minute of his existence. Clumsy and awkward, he did everything the other way around: he broke the dishes, salted the soup, smoked the milk and confused the simplest things. At first, when she picked him up, he had put her through a lot of embarrassment, calling her, in front of the visitors, mother, instead of mistress as she had expressly and strictly commanded.

He was always late preparing lunch, at every meal, at the cleaning of the cutlery. At night it was a triumph to get him not to fall asleep before eleven o'clock, the time when the old uncle used to go to bed and as the poor uncle, because of his rheumatism, could not undress himself, he necessarily needed the help of the orphan who fulfilled this obligation with a very bad will. And just as it was necessary to appeal to the boy to keep him awake after the prayers, the fight that had to be fought in the morning so that he would get up to light a fire and prepare breakfast was no less hard fought. In short, according to the heartbroken lady, it was not a calamity but a plague of calamities that had been brought into her home with the boy. And that she, as a good teacher, did not let him pass any... committed a fault, she punished it immediately; but it was such the arrogance that boasted the incorrigible stubborn child, that many times she had whipped him with all her strength without getting him to exhale an ouch or a complaint. With each blow he became paler and paler, until he became as white as a piece of paper. And that was it. A most hardened creature she had never seen nor expected to see another like it in the rest of her life!

Doña Encarnación, with her thick cheeks swollen and her eyes wet with the emotion produced by the undeserved misfortune of her beloved neighbor and friend, interrupted her at every moment to say, amidst drowned exclamations of astonishment and anger:

–Jesus, what a rogue! In my hands, little daughter, he was to fall!

And when Doña Benigna had finished, she embraced her effusively, whispering between kisses and tears:

–What a saint's patience! I am going to pray to Our Lady so that the angels may relieve you of this cross, poor little martyr!

* * *

In the kitchen Gabriel is coming and going with his small, silent steps. The blackened walls of soot underline the anemic pallor of his face, from which the roses of joy and health disappeared some time ago.

Although his stature –he is twelve years old– is inferior to that of a child of normal development, the whole of his body is harmonious and all in him predisposes people from the first moment in his favor.

However, there is something that clashes in this countenance of expression so soft, shy and sweet. The brown eyes, enlarged and bluish under-eye circles, have a scary, dazed, restless look. And from his childlike face, from his dull pupils, from his mouth without smiles, a silent protest seems to be perennially exhaled, a mute and desperate call for help that nobody hears and that never is uttered.

The sweeping and cleaning of the floor and the cleaning of the dishes are over. On a board attached to the wall, the cookware stands out burnished and shining, and the pyramids of plates shine their immaculate whiteness on the table.

The little one, after taking a look around all the corners to see if everything is in order, takes a piece of soap and a basin from the table and goes out to the patio, in which, in front of the door, there is a huge vat full of water. He extracts a quantity of the liquid and, kneeling on the floor, proceeds to wash his hands and face.

Beside the kitchen, which is the last in the series, there is a row of small rooms and, at right angles to them, two rooms and a passageway overlooking the street. A corridor with red brick tiles surrounds the entire length of the building, which is quite old and deteriorated by time.

It is nap time and the beautiful December sun illuminates the courtyard with its white, blinding light.

Sitting in the corridor, with his hands on his knees and his bust resting on one of the pillars, Gabriel receives the ardent caress of the star, still and immobile, like the post that supports him.

His shaved head, his bare feet and the coarse cloth garment he wears show clearly the kind of servitude to which he is subjected.

No noise comes from outside to disturb the serene peace of this peaceful corner. Only the buzzing of a bee or a dragonfly, as they take flight from the little garden in the center of the courtyard, interrupts, from time to time, this silent recollection.

Little by little, under the enervating influence of the environment, the little one's eyes, which were absorbed with the nostalgia of a caged bird in the wide space of the sky, began to close in. Overwhelmed with sleep, the eyelids, dragged by the weight of the long eyelashes, were falling slowly on the dark pupils until covering them completely.

Suddenly, inside one of the pieces, a high-pitched voice uttered imperious:

–Gabriel!

A shudder shook the sleeper; his eyes struggled to open; but he continued motionless.

–Gabriel! –Again the voice repeats with an accent of impatience and anger.

This time the little one wakes up startled, gets up with a jump and rushes to Mrs. Benigna's bedroom.

In front of a marble-covered hairdresser, the mistress is finishing her meticulous headdress. His face, which is reflected by the moon of the mirror, bears a marked seal of hardness and impassibility. Her complexion, very white, appears worn and full of spots and, under the scarce eyebrows, the brown eyes, small, shine penetrating, cold and scrutinizing. The salient chin, the big mouth, of thin lips, and the aquiline nose, accentuate in their physiognomy the features of an imperious and irritable character.

In spite of the fact that she has passed forty years of age, not a single gray hair whitens his black and smooth hair. Thick, of regular stature, their movements are alive, agile and reveal great energy and resolution.

A widow in her thirties, without children, very devout, the childhood has never aroused any sympathy in her, despite which she enjoys in the village a reputation as a childhood's friend, which makes her extremely proud.

As she spreads a thin layer of blush over her cheeks, she never ceases to scold the orphan who, shy and self-conscious, remains silent at the doorway.

–I have not seen deafness like yours; every time I call you, I almost shout the house down! One day I'll grab the firepick from the chimney and pierce with it those tin ears of yours!

In the bedroom, besides the comb and the bed, a wide iron cot with bronze ornaments, there is a chest of drawers with veneers and a walnut wardrobe. An old carpet of discolored shades covers the floor and on the walls, upholstered in light blue paper, numerous images of saints can be seen. At the head of the bed, and above the photograph of her late husband, hangs from a nail a small ivory crucifix.

Doña Benigna, while fixing the folds of the mantle in front of the mirror, instructs Gabriel on what to do during his absence.

–Hey, listen carefully to what I'm going to tell you. After you've made the beds and arranged the bedrooms, you sweep the rooms, the dining room and the patio. Then you start to split wood and carry water from the well to change the pot, filling it well so that it doesn't dry out in the sun. At four o'clock, you light a fire in the kitchen and heat water in the teapot and in the large pan. Then peel the potatoes and roast a little coffee for lunch. You know that the uncle is very delicate and demanding. Don't burn it like the other day. Did you understand what I said?

–Yes, mistress.

Before going out, the lady took one last look at the mirror; and after contemplating herself from the front and in profile, she left the room and headed towards the passageway.

Already in the corridor, she stopped and taking an imposing attitude she addressed the orphan with a commanding accent, remarking each of her words with her index finger raised high.

–Beware that you fall asleep and stop doing something of what I have commanded you! And do not come to me with apologies: that you lacked time; that you forgot; that your head hurt! You will not fool me, pretending to be sick. I assure you, not even dead will you be spared, because I am capable of resuscitating you with the help of sticks. So you know: no whining, no apologies: Have you heard?

–Yes, mistress.

In front of the screen she turned to make one last recommendation:

–The doors are closed. Don't let the cat come in and break a glass on top of the sideboard.

When the rumor of her steps on the pavement of the sidewalk was extinguished. Gabriel, standing in the middle of the bedroom, glanced around, mentally reviewing the orders he had just received.

As the uncle was also absent, he was alone and a prisoner in the house, because Mrs. Benigna never forgot, when she left, to double turn the lock on the street door.

For a moment the orphan experienced an irresistible desire to lie down in bed and satisfy that imperious need for sleep that tormented him. But the sight of the whip, thrown on the carpet, gave him strength to overcome such dangerous temptation.

With a resigned countenance, he went to the door on his right and entered the old man's bedroom. The room was very dark, and the vague silhouette of the bed, placed in the center of the room, was barely discernible. The little boy, who had closed the door behind him, groped toward one of the windows and opened one of the closed shutters fully, pushing the curtain aside.

A lively clarity flooded the room, the furniture of which consisted of a wardrobe, a washbasin, a bedside table, and a shabby, wide black Moroccan armchair. The poplar floor, with dust covers of raulí[1], was very old and was partly perforated by mice.

Gabriel, half-hidden behind the window, looks attentively through the crystals at the narrow, deserted alley. On the front sidewalk, in a modest-looking house, through the opening of a window whose casements are open, in the interior of a small room, at the back of it, a bed with pink hangings can be seen.

For a few minutes, he did not separate his sight from the solitary room, until, making a visible effort, he moved away from the window to begin the task of fixing the bed, putting in order sheets and blankets with feminine tidiness.

When he had finished, fatigued by the effort, he leaned on the edge of the bed and with his arms down and his head somewhat inclined, he remained motionless in a meditative attitude.

Little by little his face, which reflected his thoughts, acquired a painful expression of bitterness. The tenacious memories of the past assailed him again, showing him by yesterday's contrast how painful the present is and how bleak the future is.

Again, the happy days at home and at school, and the days of mourning and pain that followed, the tragic death of his father, victim of an accident in a mechanic's workshop, and the death of his mother who, unable to bear the fatigue of excessive work, was to meet her beloved husband in the cemetery, two months later, paraded through his brain in endless procession.

Gabriel seems to be pleased to evoke these cruel events, shredding their smallest details. He forgets nothing; he goes from one fact to another without stopping, until the memory of his twin sisters is vivid in his imagination. Two years younger than him, very alive and funny, the little ones appeared to him in that instant as she saw them six months ago.

And, suddenly, the scene of the separation from his sisters arose in his spirit, producing such a sharp sensation of pain that, in order to drive it away, he gathered all the energies of his will. But, in spite of his efforts, the vision was so precise in his brain that it was impossible for him to remove the most insignificant detail from his memory.

...With what desperate cries the little ones hugged each other at his neck, when the guardian appointed by the judge wanted to take them to the car waiting at the door of the mortuary house! He still seemed to hear their wails and their heart-wrenching cries, as they were pulled out by force, from his arms, and still saw their convulsed and terrified faces peeping out

---

1 *Nothofagus alpina* tree.

of the carriage door, calling him frantically: –Gabriel, don't leave us; come, Gabriel!

He threw a muffled groan, and in an access of desperation he let himself fall on his face in the bed, hiding in the bed clothes his face bathed in tears and muttering quietly between sobs:

–Dad, daddy, why did you die! Mom, where are you!

Suddenly he stood up to look at an object suspended on the wall, above the bedside table.

After contemplating it attentively for a moment, he took his tearful eyes away from it, discouraged. No, he would never dare! And as he remembered the details of his first attempt, this conviction was accentuated in him.

When he seized the gun that last time, taking it out of its leather case, he had obeyed one of those blind and unconscious impulses that sometimes attacked him in his hours of solitude. With the anguish of a shipwrecked man who grabs a burning iron, he had taken the revolver and twice rested its muzzle on his temples. He remembered how he the trigger gave up under the pressure of his fingers, but when only a very small extra pressure was required to let the shot go, a sensation that he could not understand had suddenly paralyzed his muscles. It was not the fear of physical torture, nor of death, but the fear of the detonation that had cowed him. Ah! if the shot went off without a sound, if the bullet had penetrated silently into his flesh, no reflection would have stopped him, he was sure of it.

And how sweet it would be for him to die! He was so miserable! He was so alone, so helpless against the cruel rigors of fate! And never a friendly face, a kind voice, a compassionate look that would comfort and encourage him to endure his endless ordeal!

Ah, if she had not appeared, in spite of his repugnance, he would have tried again to end once and for all such a miserable existence!

That unforgettable moment, when passing in front of that window, he heard someone inside utter inside with a very sweet accent:

–Poor thing, he's so beaten!

He raised his face and glimpsed a white face and in it two blue eyes that looked at him with tender commiseration.

That, for him, divine apparition, was like a ray of light in the darkness of his despair; but, as he came out rarely, he seldom saw her and every time this happened, he was prey of a strange disturbance. A mixture of inexplicable joy, fear and shame seized his spirit, and his shyness was such that one day, when he found her in the street, he was on the point of releasing the wine carafe he was carrying in his hand. A burning blush burned into his face and, horrified by himself, by his shaven head, his bare feet, and his vile and dirty suit, he returned home with desolation in his soul.

Soon he had the absolute assurance that she was also unhappy and that, like him, she was alone in the world, without parents or relatives, without siblings. The melancholic expression of his countenance, the mourning of his costume and that sad song that she sometimes sang and whose melody he learned by heart, clearly stated it.

Yes, he was not the only one who was alone. There, a few steps away, was someone who also suffered from the same evil, and suffered the same martyrdom.

And this link that the misfortune tied between them, was so precious to him that such single memory was sometimes enough to make him forget for an instant his bitter tribulations.

To this selfish feeling were also added other contradictory ones, whose essence he was incapable of understanding. One afternoon, when he thought she was fixing her eyes on a boy from the neighborhood, he felt that a very sharp pain, so strange in its nature, was piercing his heart; he was filled with confusion when he wanted to analyze the strange phenomenon.

His greatest pleasure was to contemplate her from there, without her noticing him, through the crystals, abruptly moving away and closing the shutter when the blue pupils were fixed in that direction.

As Gabriel glimpses behind the window casements in his neighbor's room, a graceful figure suddenly enters it.

She is a young girl between the ages of fourteen and fifteen, dressed in a modest and elegant black cashmere suit. In her virgin face, with its purest lines, there is a sweet and serene expression, with no hints of melancholy. Blonde, slender, with a mother-of-pearl complexion, with beautiful blue eyes, she appears before Gabriel, who looks at her static, like one of those enchanted princesses that the wonderful stories of geniuses and necromancers tell about.

Leaning on the balcony, she gazes distractedly into the lonely alleyway, when suddenly a blond boy looking like a student on holiday suddenly appears behind her, and taking her by the waist, lifts her from the floor and undertakes a series of twists and turns around the room. She screams and laughs until tears are shed and when, finally, she succeeds in getting rid of him, she in turn takes the offensive, linking the aggressor's neck with her snowy arms. He resists as much as he can the shaking of that body that twists around his and both laugh like madmen.

Suddenly, the gentle pugilist ceases in her games and says to her brother with alarm tone:

–Pedro, have you heard?

–Yes, it looks like a door that the wind slammed shut.

* * *

The first thing that caught Mrs. Benigna's attention when she returned to her home was the great silence that reigned in the house and above all in the kitchen. She entered the latter, and her surprise, seeing the fire completely extinguished, had no limits; but, very soon, astonishment yielded the field to anger, which awoke in her fiercely. She went out into the courtyard and shrieked in anger:

–Gabriel, where are you? Gabriel!

Suddenly she fell silent and went quietly to the orphan's room. A sudden idea had illuminated his brain: the very lazy one, she thought, has reclined on the bed and has fallen asleep.

But a new setback awaited her there, for the room was empty. Then she went to the dining room and, as she crossed this room, she saw with growing indignation that he had not done the usual cleaning. But where her courage reached its peak was when she contemplated the disarrangement of her bedroom. Her choleric glances stumbled upon the little whip, whose grip she seized, heading, with it on her right hand, towards the uncle's room. When she opened the door, her obsession to surprise the delinquent in fraganti was such that she hardly noticed the pungent smell of the room.

Her first glance was towards the bed, her eyes immediately resting on the armchair in which the silhouette of the sleeper stood out, immersed in a vague gloom. She tiptoed towards him, and when she stood beside him, she poured a rain of furious lashes over the motionless figure, as she screamed in frenzied rage:

–Take, you rascal, you lazy, rascal!

Suddenly, his arm stopped suddenly; something liquid dropping from the whip had splashed on her face and, taking a step towards the window, she opened the shutters violently.

Along with the clarity that flooded the room, Mrs. Benigna's countenance became the most faithful image of terror. Her eyes opened disproportionately; her knees flinched; the blood clotted her brain and, slipping into something viscous, she collapsed into the floor.

Minutes later, a cat with white and shiny fur moved silently towards the same place in the bedroom and stopped at something damp on the floor. He watched the obstacle attentively, approached it with his pink nose and, suddenly, with the disrespect that characterizes those of his race, jumped on the inert back of his owner and from there to the window sill, where he sat comfortably next to the crystals.

From time to time, with an ironic and contemptuous expression, he fixed his green pupils on that child with a waxy face, with his head reclined at an angle on the armchair in which he is seated, and on the shapeless and voluminous body of the mistress, lying on her face, on the ground, with the red whip on her right hand and her head between those bare feet that hang white, rigid, and under which a wide purple tapestry extends.

The Attached Hand

On the dusty road, overwhelmed by fatigue and the gleaming radiance of the sun, Don Paico, the old vagabond with his attached hand, walks. His bony right hand oppresses a thick cane on which he rests his angular, stark body, from whose narrow shoulders the long neck bends flaccidly under the weight of the round, bare head, like a billiard ball.

A hat of earthy, greasy cloth, with hanging wings, sunk to the ears, half veils his face of indefinable expression, a mixture of cunning and simplicity, animated by two tearful eyes that flicker without ceasing. A long faded blanket full of patches falls in heavy folds, almost reaching his knees, and his bare feet that crawl as he walks leave behind him a wide furrow in the thick layer of dust that covers the road.

Next to him, mounted on a chestnut horse of magnificent appearance, rides don Simón Antonio, and further back, some riders in agile cavalcades, follow their master at a respectful distance: the butler and a cattleman of the ranch.

The atmosphere is suffocating. The air is motionless and a scorching breath seems to come from those flat and arid lands, cut in all directions by adobe walls, living hedges and the fences of the pastures.

Don Simón Antonio with his big palm hat, held by a silk chinstrap and his threaded mantle with blue stripes, also seems to feel the enervating influence of that environment. His wide, blushing face is damp, sweaty; and their grey eyes, ordinarily so lively and sparkling in the gloom of their droopy eyebrows, now look dull, sleepy and drowsy.

Leaning over the saddle, he holds the reins with his left hand and presses with his right hand the whip with a bamboo handle and a silver knob, an inseparable companion of his person, which, as a weapon of attack and defense or an instrument of torture, is always ready to crack in his vigorous fist.

Suddenly don Simón Antonio comes out of his drowsiness, restrains the horse and, steeped in the stirrups, hits the old man legs with his whip, who, surprised, wobbles, hesitates and looks frightened around him.

The butler and the cattleman, at the sight of the vagabond's forced pirouettes, smile and whisper, while the master, again hoisting the whip, shouts with his thick bass voice:

–Come on, quick, old thief!

Don Paico strives to accelerate the pace. From his feet rises a cloud of dust that drowns him, tearing from his chest a harsh noise, like the sound of broken bellows. His big nose is aquiline, sharp, falling vertically on the toothless mouth, with thin lips, which gives a sly and astute look to the withered countenance, shaded by a scarce grey beard, tangled and dirty.

That prisoner, victim of the wrath of Don Simon Antonio, is an old beggar who travels the fields and villages in the hot summer days, imploring public charity. His popularity is immense among the peasants, who never get tired of hearing him tell the story of his attached hand, of that hand, the sinister hand, that the vagabond carries attached to the flesh under his right nipple and that, according to fame, cannot be detached from there, because at the slightest attempt in that sense the blood jumps as if a knife was tearing his skin.

Therefore, when, in the middle of the peace of the fields, under the sun that burns the hills and exhausts the grass in the yellow meadows, one sees the curved silhouette of the old man appear suddenly in a bend of the road, the boys abandon their games and run to meet them, shouting:

–Don Paico, here comes Don Paico, the one with the attached hand!

And men and women from all over rush to meet the newcomer. Everyone, grandparents and grandchildren, old and young, do their best to entertain the old man, offering him bread, fruits and toasted wheat flour. And then, when the walker has postponed hunger and thirst, there is never a lack of one who says with a tone of supplication:

–Now, Don Paico, tell us about it.

The old man squints his eyes and pauses for a thoughtful moment to gather his memories, and then, looking for the most comfortable position on the rustic bench, he begins with his cascading and monotonous voice, in the midst of the avid silence of the auditorium, the invariable narration that each one, by force of hearing it repeated, already knows by heart.

–Yes, I remember as if it were today. It was a day like this. The sun was sparking up there and it seemed that it was going to set fire to the dry pastures and stubble. I and others my age had taken off our jackets and played hopscotch under the branches of the trees. At that time my beard was barely appearing in my face and I was a well planted strong boy, straight as a spindle, a cockerel for the beautiful girls.

Here the narrator interrupted himself to make his tongue snap and inspect the chubby faces of the girls who burst off laughing. The old man waited with comical gravity, until the laughs were extinguished and then he went on:

–My mother, the poor old woman, had the living genius and the hand too ready to rub our ribs with the stick or the whip if we were not ready to obey her. Twice that day she had already shouted at me from the kitchen door:

–Pascual, bring me some dry splinters to light the oven!

I, blinded by the demon of the game, answered her, following with my eyes the flight of the copper rings:

–I'm coming, Mother, I'm coming.

But the devil had grabbed me and I wasn't going, I wasn't going...

Suddenly, when, with the ring in my hand and my body in tension, I put my five senses to plant a double in the line, I felt in my back a blow and a sting as if a burning iron had come at me. I gave a snort and, blind with rage, like a beast that pounces fiercely, I released a backhand blow with my left hand with all my strength.

I heard a scream, a cloud darkened the sight and I glimpsed my mother who, without letting go of the whip, straightened herself on the floor with her face full of blood, at the same time as she shouted at me with a voice that froze me to death:

–Damned, damned son!

I felt the world coming upon me and I fell round. When I came back I had my left hand, the sacrilegious hand, stuck under my right nipple.

The story always ended in deep silence. The bystanders, with their eyes fixed on the narrator, listened to his words with a religious anointing and, when he had finished, they were amazed by that prodigy, whose evidence was there in front of their eyes.

The women crossed themselves and groaned:

–Blessed be God! Poor thing!

After the first impression, the tongues were loosened and some timid voices were uttered:

–Now, don Paico, let's see that.

And the circle was whirling, becoming compact. The shortest ones steeped in the tips of their feet and the children shrieked attached to the clothes of their mothers:

–Me, me too, take me up!

Then the old man opened the folds of his mantle and half opened his dirty shirt, showing to the avid glances his sunken, skinny chest, with the skin attached to the bones. And there, just below the nipple, was the hand, a pale hand with long fingers and huge fingernails, attached by the palm to that part of the body as if it was welded or sewn into it.

Then, in order to demonstrate the solidity of that adherence, he took the paralyzed limb with his right hand and swirled it as if trying to detach it. And then, oh prodigy! As a visible sign of divine anger, the back of the hand reddened and the frightened women shouted in chorus:

–Oh God, he's bleeding! Most Holy Virgin!

And all them crossed themselves.

Don Simon Antonio, who is exasperated by the slow march of his prisoner, harasses him at every moment, cracking his whip and shouting with an irritated voice:

–Come on, hurry up, you great rascal!

It's lunchtime and he feels a voracious appetite. From time to time he rises above the stirrups and extends above the walls a scrutinizing glance, look of master, satisfied and distrustful at the same time. All those lands, as far as the eye can see, belong to him, making him one of the wealthiest landowners in the region.

That morning he was walking through his fields as usual, when suddenly his penetrating sight distinguished the old man who was crossing one of the paddocks, looking everywhere with a restless air, like a thief. Immediately he nailed the spurs to the horse and closed the passage giving him the order to follow him to the houses of the estate. The beggar, very frightened, did not make any observation and began to walk in silence next to the chestnut of Don Simon Antonio. It had been a long time since the patron had wished for such an encounter, for in his capacity as judge of that district, he had longed to make an exemplary example of the person of that loafer who exploited the credulity of the people with that ridiculous hoax of the attached hand.

The trickery used by the old man to make a living filled him with indignation. That fraud was a robbery, an iniquitous robbery, all the more odious because the victims of that plunder were poor peasants, ignorant and credulous, who accepted in good faith the crude inventions of that cunning impostor.

Don Simón Antonio owed his fortune, partly to his indefatigable tenacity to treasure it and partly to certain actions that several times were made public, and for that reason some rumors about his probity begun to spread, rumors that, without taking away his sleep, mortified him more than he had confessed on this particular matter.

When he was appointed judge of that rural district, he saw in the exercise of the office a means of closing the mouth to the ones who spread such rumors. He would show such a great love for justice; he would display such an ardor to pursue evil that his fame as an upright magistrate would blot out, he was sure of it, the sins he was blamed for.

And consistent with this purpose, he became a relentless persecutor of marauders, beggars, vagabonds, and whatever poor devil seemed suspicious to him. In his obsession to see criminals everywhere, the slightest fault acquired in his eyes the proportions of a crime whose punishment executed by his own hand sometimes endowed characteristics of savage cruelty.

The legend of the old man, which he qualified as a gross mystification, exalted his anger and he had given strict orders to his servants to seize the criminal and bring him into his presence. But the peasants, in spite of their fear of the master, had not dared to fulfill their mandates, and the vagabond, warned of the danger had until then avoided as far as possible approaching the domains of the severe and implacable judge.

A great terror had taken hold of the wretched man's spirit and he was walking as fast as he could, suffering without complaining the lashes that the impatient Simón Antonio was shaking on his shoulders. What did that terrible man want from him? He wanted to disappear beneath the earth swallowed by that dust in which his bare, wide and deformed feet sank wearily.

And the road, limited to the right and left by the high adobe walls, stretched forward and backward of the small retinue, solitary, monotonous and endless. The rays of the sun plummeted on its calcined reflective surface. In the dry, scorching air, the dust raised by the horses' hoofs floated, forming a curtain behind the riders' backs that hid the road they had traveled.

At last, after a bend, the large iron fence that led to the farmhouses suddenly appeared. A moment later the beggar and his captors were in the vast courtyard in front of the sumptuous façade of the building. Don Simón Antonio handed over his horse to a groom and ordered that the prisoner should be taken to the dungeon. The old man, until then, had allowed himself to be led meekly, quietly, without the slightest resistance, undoubtedly hoping that his sweetness and shyness would soften the hearts of his captors. But, in spite of everything, on his face there was an expression of fear, of awe that, suddenly, at the sight of the trap: a long iron bar with its corresponding rings placed horizontally in a corner of the cell, became a mad terror, and without being able to contain himself groaned, addressing Simon Antonio:

–What are you going to do with me, Master?

For only answer, the landowner put his thick hand on the old man's shoulder and said to him:

–Let's see, take off your mantle.

Don Paico, with the same pitiful tone, replied:

–I can't, sir, I can't.

Then the formidable right hand leaned on him and knocked him down how long he was on the pavement. And as he debated uselessly to get rid of the terrible pressure, he heard the master command:

–Secure his feet.

When the sound of the irons had been extinguished, the prisoner found himself lying on his back in the hard earth, his legs held high by his ankles. He had been stripped of his blanket and only kept his trousers and old shirt.

The boss, after wiping away the sweat that flooded his rubicund face, stood up with all the majesty of his corpulent person and wielding the terrible whip, began the interrogation:

–You are going to begin by telling me how long you have been deceiving people with this infamous trickery of the sticking hand.

The old man implored:

–It is not deceit, master, I swear by the wounds of Our Lord.

Don Simón Antonio roared in a stentorian voice:

–Ah, so it's not a lie, bandit, thief!

And bowing down, he took the delinquent's shirt and tore it off in small tatters. The peasants, who were watching the scene from a certain distance, approached a few steps with an expression of fear and curiosity. The vagabond, naked to the waist, made futile efforts to straighten up. At the lack of clarity that filtered through the lattice window, his fleshy skeletal body appeared in all its horrible physiological misery. While the right hand rested on the ground, the left hand remained attached by the palm to the rough skin of the chest.

The landowner, ignoring the old man's lamentations, grabbed his hand by the wrist and pulled it brutally. The prisoner exhaled a groan, made a last effort to get up and then remained still, fixing an anxious look on Don Simón Antonio, who, with a triumphal smile, verified that in the place where that member was supported there was not even the remotest sign of adherence. The skin was there whiter, softer; that was all.

–I knew it –he exclaimed after a moment, releasing the arm that its owner in vain tried to hide from the avid eyes that gazed at him. And turning to the peasants his radiant face, rejoicing that he had unmasked the impostor, he said to them, pointing with his right hand to the bare chest of the beggar:

–You see, there's no such thing as glue, welding or anything like it here. Everything is nothing but a farce of this rascal to be able to live without working.

Then he ordered two stakes to be nailed to the ground, one on each side of the prisoner, to which he fastened a rope around his wrists. Backwards, arms open, in the posture of the crucified, the old man turned from his stupor began to throw pitiful ayes:

–Oh, master, kill me better!

At the end of that first part of their work, Don Simón Antonio went to his rooms for lunch, leaving to his butler the task of summoning the tenants so that they would be convinced by their own eyes of the deception that for so long made them victims of that false invalid vagabond.

At the ringing of the bell, whose clear ringing slipped through the scorching air through the fields, the peasants came in small groups, whispering to each other in a low and fearful voice. Once in the dungeon they fixed their frightened eyes on the prisoner who continued to moan in his weak, mournful voice.

–Oh, Lord, have mercy on this poor old man!

None spoke, but in their weathered faces pity could be guessed. And then that big punishment did not convince them. Because, if the hand was now free, loosened, for them it simply meant that the punishment brought by the maternal curse had been fulfilled and that the justice of God was satisfied with the penitence of the criminal. And to his eyes the mournful figure of the old man appeared surrounded by the halo of the saint, of the martyr. They contemplated that spectacle for a moment and withdrew in silence, carrying in their hearts a deaf anger against the patron who thus defied the wrath of God.

At the end of lunch, Simón Antonio appeared again in the courtyard, and approaching the chestnut that a servant had from the bridle, he put his foot on the stirrup and hoisted himself laboriously over the saddle. His thick cheeks, red from the libations, and the brightness of his eyes reflected the excitement produced by the feast he had enjoyed. He had some satisfaction with the justice in hand, and he had no doubt that the matter was going to have some resonance, for it was not a matter of vulgar pettiness but of the exploits of a seasoned malefactor who for years had emptied people's pockets into the very noses of the authority, and surely would have continued to empty them if he had not been there to prevent it, discovering the deception that the criminal used for his purposes. Convicted and confessed the delinquent, the only thing left to do was to apply the penalty to him. Don Simón Antonio meditated on the point for a moment and immediately gave an order to untie the prisoner and bring him to his presence.

Under the compassionate gaze of the peasants who silently stepped aside to give way, the old man appeared with his head bowed and his countenance pale with anxiety and fear. When he was two steps away from the horse, he lifted his face and groaned:

–Pardon me, master, I beg your pardon!

Don Simón Antonio glanced with majesty around the surroundings and then, with a low and belligerent tone, he began to speak.

As a "constituted authority, he had a painful duty to fulfill": that of doing justice, giving each one his own and punishing the wicked with the full force of the law. This man had, for many years, deceived the good faith of the people in order to take away their food and clothing by means of a gross trickery, which allowed him to live like a drone without working. That was a crime, a crime which he, the representative of justice, could not allow to go unpunished. There was, therefore, a lesson to be made of that vagabond, which would serve as an example and a healthy warning to young and old, without exception.

A deep silence followed his words, only the old man's mournful song could be heard:

–Excuse me, friend, excuse me!

Then the face of Simón Antonio was clothed with the august gravity of the judge who issued his ruling without appeal. His imposing voice resounded:

–You will immediately leave the district of my jurisdiction. Woe to you if I find you again in these places! I will skin you alive.

He paused and added:

–But before we separate, you are going to carry a souvenir of me.

And stepping on his stirrups, he hoisted the heavy whip.

The old man, who had started to walk towards the gate, was suddenly enveloped in such a rain of lashes, that more than a human cry it was a beast's roar that sprouted from his throat. And as the whip whistled on his back, twisting around his body like a snake, the sufferer fell and rose, exhaling the hoarse cry without interruption:

–Sorry, master, sorry, master!

The peasants witnessed the punishment quiet and motionless like statues, jaws clenched, white teeth between their trembling lips.

At last, Don Simón Antonio dropped his strong arm. The old man lay on the ground like a fallen frog, curled up, facing the earth. His bald white, naked, head shone under the sun, whose glaring flame stung the tanned faces of the peasants like an ember of fire.

One last detail was still missing for justice to be fulfilled, and, at a sign from the patron, the butler and the cowboy lifted up the beggar, and stretching their arms they tied them along a wooden rod that crossed his back at shoulder level. Immediately the old man who had not opened his mouth during this operation, convinced of the futility of his pleas, started walking with his head down and arms crossed towards the gate, followed by the compassionate glances of the farmers.

–José –commanded to the cattleman Don Simón Antonio–, take him along the royal road so that everyone may see this scoundrel and know the deception he was doing. Once out of the farm, you shake some whips on him so that he doesn't feel like coming back here.

And while the vagabond continued his very long ordeal along the road, the landowner turned to the butler and quietly asked him:

–Did they come for the cows this morning?

–Yes, sir.

–And did they not notice the change?

–Nothing, sir; they came in a hurry and just herded them.

Don Simón Antonio was thoughtful for a while, calculating what those four consumptive cows which he used to replace other four healthy ones, reported him of profit, besides the price paid, in view of the good quality of the cattle, by the incautious buyer. And the result of the calculation must have been flattering, because he threw a grunt of satisfaction, and even smiled slightly when, as he looked towards the road, he perceived through the grille the comic and ominous figure of the old man, advancing in front of the cattle man, with open arms, as if behind those shadows of justice and mercy, under the ironic gaze of the sun.

Cañuela and Petaca

As Petaca glimpses from the door, Cañuela, perched on the table, picks up the heavy, moldy rifle from the wall.

The joyful rays of the sun filtering through the thousand slits of the ranch spread a dazzling clarity inside the house.

Both boys are alone that morning. Old Pedro and his wife, elderly Rosalía, Cañuela's grandparents, left very early in the direction of town, after recommending to their grandson the greatest circumspection during his absence.

Cañuela, in spite of his lack of strength –he is nine years old, and his body is slanted and thin– has happily finished the enterprise of seizing the weapon, and sitting on the edge of the bed, with the barrel between his legs, with the butt resting on the ground, he examines the terrible instrument with serious attention and care. His bleached blond hair, and his clear eyes of impassive and candid gaze contrast remarkably with Petaca's blackened and hirsute hair and dark and vivacious eyes, who, two years older than his cousin, of short and chubby body, is the antithesis of Cañuela, whom he handles and governs with despotic authority.

That project of hunting was caressed by them since some time ago, the object of mysterious meetings and deliberations; but, they had always found difficulties, insurmountable inconveniences, that impeded them from carrying it out. How to provide gunpowder, pellets and percussion caps? Finally, one afternoon, while Cañuela watched the pot of tea over the embers of the home, he suddenly saw the furtive and silent figure of Petaca appear in the doorway, who, upon learning that the old people were not yet returning from the village, placed before Cañuela's astonished eyes a thick bag of gunpowder for mines that he had hidden under his clothes. The acquisition of the explosive was a whole story that his hero did not take care to tell, enraptured in the contemplation of that glistening substance similar to polished jet.

Within a league of the ranch was a quarry that supplied neighboring villages with building materials. Petaca's father was the foreman of those works. Every morning he extracted the provision of gunpowder for the day from the deposit excavated in the living rock. In vain the boy had put into play the mischief and subtlety of his ingenuity to seize one of those bags that the old man had next to him in the small tent, from which he directed the work. All his cunning and stratagems had unfortunately failed before the alert eyes that watched his movements. Desperate to obtain his object, he finally tried a heroic measure. He had observed that when a shot was ready, given the danger signal, the workers, even the foreman, always went to take shelter in a hole, opened for that purpose on the side of the mountain, and did not leave there until the explosion had taken place. One morning, crawling like a snake, he lay in wait near the tent. Very soon, three blows with a hammer in a steel drill announced that the fuse of a shot had just been lit and he saw his father and the stonemasons running to hide in the excavation. That was the right time, and rushing over the gunpowder sacks he seized one, and immediately started a fast race, jumping like a goat over the piles of stone which, in a great extension, covered the slope of the mountain. When the explosion that shook the ground beneath his feet occurred, enormous projectiles buzzed in his ears, bouncing around him a furious hailstorm of hailstones. But none touched him, and when the stonemasons left his hiding place, he was already far away pressing his glorious conquest against his panting chest, filling his soul with joy.

That afternoon, which was a Thursday, it was agreed that the hunt would be the following Sunday, the day they could dispose of as they pleased; since the grandparents would be absent, as usual, to bring their birds and vegetables to the market. In the meantime, the gunpowder had to be hidden. Many hiding places were proposed and discarded. None seemed safe enough for such a treasure. Cañuela proposed that a hole be opened in a corner of the garden to hid it there, but his cousin dissuaded him by telling him that a boy, a neighbor of his, had done the same with a sack of those, finding days later only the paper wrap. All the contents had been spoiled by the moisture. So they had to look for a dry place. And while they were trying uselessly to solve that problem, The silly Cañuela, who, according to his cousin, never thought of anything to his advantage, said, suddenly, pointing to the fire burning in the middle of the room:

–Let's bury it in the ashes!

Petaca looked at him in admiration, and by a rare exception, because what his cousin proposed was always detestable to him, he was going to accept that time when the sight of the fire stopped him: what if it is lit? he thought. Suddenly he leapt for joy. He had found the solution. In an instant both boys removed the embers and ashes from the fireplace and dug a hole forty centimeters deep in the middle of the fireplace, inside which, wrapped in a handful of herbs, they placed the gunpowder bag covering it with the extracted earth and returning to its place the fire over which the chipped clay pot was again placed.

In half an hour everything was beautifully finished, and Petaca retired promising his cousin that the pellets and the percussion caps would be in his possession before Sunday.

During the days that preceded the indicated one, Cañuela did not cease to think of the possibility of an explosion that may overturn the pot of the snack, leaving him and his grandparents without supper, that was the only serious consequence he imagined. And this sinister thought grew stronger when he saw his grandmother Rosalía inflating her cheeks and blowing briskly, stoking the fire, which, incidentally, without knowing, that a whole Vesuvius was there in front of her noses, ready to make its unexpected and fulminating appearance. When this happened, Cañuela stood on tiptoes and slid towards the door, glancing back sideways and mumbling with a restless air:

–Now it's bursting, damn it!

But it didn't burst, and the boy calmed down until he discarded all fear.

And when Sunday arrived and the old people, with their load on the slope disappeared in the distance, on the mountain path, the boys, radiant with joy, began the preparations for the expedition. Petaca had fulfilled his word by stealing from his father a load of percussion caps and, as for the pellets, they had been replaced with great advantage and economy by small pebbles collected in the bed of the stream.

Having unearthed the gunpowder that both found, after touching it, perfectly dry and warm, and carefully examining the grandfather's rifle, as venerable and ancient as its owner, there was nothing left but to undertake the march towards the hills and stubble, which they did after properly securing the door of the ranch. Forward, with his rifle on his shoulder, was Petaca, followed closely by Cañuela, who carried the munitions of war in the wide pockets of his breeches. For a moment they disputed about the path they should follow. Cañuela was of opinion to descend to the ravine and continue to the valley, where they would find flocks of mockingbirds and thrushes; but his stubborn cousin wished to go rather through the stubble, where meadowlarks and partridges abounded, hunting, according to him, much superior to the other, and, as usual, his decision was the one that prevailed.

Petaca was wearing a jacket, discarded from his father, whose sleeves and lower contour had been cut to the height of the pockets, which were, with this arrangement, eliminated. Cañuela did not have a jacket and covered her chest with a shirt; but, instead, he wore her legs wrapped in thick cloth trousers, with enormous pockets that were his pride, and served, at the same time, as an ark, an arsenal and a pantry.

Petaca, with the rifle on his shoulder, was sweating and snorting under the weight of the enormous gun. Walking well erect, stretching his small body, to maintain a continent worthy of a hunter, stubbornly resisting the pleas of his cousin, who begged him to allow him to carry, even for a little while, the precious instrument.

During the first stage, Cañuela, full of hunting ardor, wanted to shot all living creatures, not forgiving even the swarms of mosquitoes that buzzed in the air. At every moment his discrete calling: hey, hey! called the attention of his companion, and when he stopped interrogating him with his sparkling eyes, he pointed with his right hand, a miserable sparrow that jumped among the grass. Facing that vile hunt, the brown Nimrod scornfully shrugged his shoulders and continued his triumphal march through the hills, bent under the rifle whose moldy barrel protruded when the butt was placed on the ground, a fourth above his head.

Finally, the unhappy hunter saw in front of him a piece worthy of the honors of a shot. A male meadowlark, whose red breast looked like a freshly opened wound, threw his cheerful song over a fence of branches. The boys fell to the ground and began to crawl like reptiles through the undergrowth. The bird watched their movements calmly and gave no signs of restlessness except when they were four steps away. Then he opened his wings and went to rest on the grass fifty meters from that place. From that moment on, a mad hunt began through the stubble. When, after great detours and infinite precautions, Petaca managed to get close enough and began to aim the weapon, the bird flew and was going to launch its scream, which seemed to be a mockery and a challenge, a hundred steps further. As if he proposed to test the constancy of his enemies, he would now cross a bush or a ravine that was difficult to access, but always in the sight of his tireless persecutors, who, after a few hours of this gymnastic exercise, were bathed in sweat, full of scratches and with their clothes made a sieve; but they were not discouraged and continued the hunt with wild ardor.

Finally, the bird, tired of such an unimportant persecution, rose into the air and, crossing a deep ravine, and disappeared into the woods of the opposite slope.

Cañuela and Petaca, who, with their hair over their eyes, were crawling along a furrow, straightened up consulting each other with their gaze, and then, without uttering a single word, went on, determined to die of fatigue rather than give up such a magnificent piece. When, after crossing the ravine, exhausted, they found another one on the hills, the first thing they saw was the fugitive, who, perched on a small bush, was destroying the tender stems of the plant with her strong beak. To see it and to fall both of them on their faces on the grass was all one. Petaca, with dazzled eyes fixed on the bird, began to crawl with his belly on the ground towing the rifle with his right hand. He was barely breathing, putting all his soul into that silent slide.

Four meters from the tree he stopped and, gathering all his exhausted strength, he threw the shotgun in his face. But the moment he was about to pull the trigger, Cañuela, who had followed him without him noticing, suddenly shouted at him with her sharp, penetrating voice:

—Wait, it's not loaded, man!

The meadowlark flapped his wings and got lost like an arrow on the horizon. Petaca jumped up, and rushing to the his blond cousin, ground it with blows and slaps. What a beast and what a brute it was! To go and scare away the hunt at the precise moment when he was going to fall infallibly dead. He had aimed the gun so well!

And when Cañuela sobbed, he stammered:

–Because I told you it wasn't loaded...!

To which the dark-haired boy replied angrily, arms in a pitcher, nailing the flaming eyes of anger to his cousin:

–Why didn't you wait for the shot?

Cañuela stopped sobbing, suddenly, and wiping his eyes with the back of his hand, he looked at Petaca, gawking, with his mouth open. How deserving were the slaps! How could he not think of something so simple? No, he had to surrender to the evidence. He was a moron, nothing more than a moron.

The harmony between the boys was soon restored. Lying in the shade of a tree they rested for a while to recover from the fatigue that overwhelmed them. Petaca, already past the access of furor, reflected and almost regretted its hardness because, in truth, to kill a bird with an unloaded shotgun no longer seemed possible to him, no matter how well he aimed. But since to confess his clumsiness would have been to agree with his idiotic cousin, he quietly kept his reflections to himself. He would have gladly given the dynamite cartridge he had there in the ranch, hidden under his bed, for having killed the damned meadowlark that had made them suffer so much. If they had loaded the gun when they left! But it was still time to repair such a capital omission, and standing up, he called Cañuela to help him in the serious and delicate operation, of which both had only vague and confused notions, because they had not yet had a chance to see how a shotgun was loaded.

And while Cañuela, perched on a trunk to dominate the extremity of the rifle that his cousin kept in an upright position, was waiting for orders, ramrod in hand, the first difficulty arose. What came first? The gunpowder or the pebbles?

Petaca, although quite perplexed, was inclined to believe that gunpowder, and was going to resolve the question in this sense, when Cañuela, coming out of his silence, timidly expressed the same idea. Petaca's spirit of intransigent contradiction against everything that came from his cousin was revealed this time as always. It was enough for the blond to propose something for him to immediately do the opposite. And with what scornful emphasis he mocked the occurrence! One needed to be more stupid than an ox to think such nonsense. If the gunpowder went first, the pebbles had to be thrown on top of it. And where did the shot come from? Not at all, they should proceed in the opposite way. Cañuela, which held his breath, fearful that one of his answers would lead to more forceful reasons on his ribs, emptied into the barrel of the weapon a respectable quantity of pebbles on which he immediately threw two thick handfuls of gunpowder. A bundle of dry grass served as a taco, and with the placement of the percussion cap, which Petaca carried out without difficulty, the rifle was ready to launch its deadly discharge. The intrepid dark-haired boy put it on his shoulder and began to walk followed by his comrade, eagerly scanning the horizon in search of a victim. Birds abounded, but they took flight as soon as the end of the rifle threatened to knock them off their pedestal in the branch. None of them had the courtesy to remain still while the hunter made and rectified his aim once and a thousand times. Finally, an imperturbable Andean sparrow was pleased, while smoothing his feathers on a branch, to wait for the end of such strange and complicated manipulations. While Petaca, who had placed his rifle on a trunk, was pointing kneeling on the grass, Cañuela, prudently placed on his back, waited, with his hands in his ears, for the sound of the shot that seemed formidable, an idea that also assaulted the hunter, remembering the shots he heard exploding in the quarry and, for a moment, hesitated without resolving to pull the trigger; But the thought that his cousin could mock his cowardice made him turn his head, close his eyes and press the trigger. Great was his surprise when he heard instead of the roar that he expected, a sharp and dry click, but there was nothing exciting about it. It seems a lie, he thought, that a shotgun sounds so little. And his first glance was for the bird, and not seeing it on the branch, he gave a shout of joy and rushed forward sure to find it on the ground, upside down.

Cañuela, who saw the Andean sparrow move away calmly, did not dare to disillusion him; and such was the heat with which his cousin pondered the precision of the shot, of how he saw the feathers fly through the air and the bird fall gutted from the branches that, forgetting what he had seen, concluded, also, by believing on fully in the death of the bird, looking for it with determination among the undergrowth until, tired of the uselessness of the investigation, they abandoned it, discouraged. But, both had smelled the gunpowder and their bellicose enthusiasm increased considerably, becoming a thirst for extermination and destruction that nothing could quench.

They quickly loaded the rifle and, having lost their fear of the weapon, they gave themselves ardently to that imaginary slaughter. The weak burst of the percussion cap maintained that illusion, and although both noticed at first with surprise the very little smoke that gunpowder emitted, they ended up not remembering that insignificant detail.

Only a contrariness clouded his joy. They could not collect a single piece, even though Petaca swore and perjured herself to have seen her fall dead and plucked, almost, by the shrapnel of the pebbles. But inside, he began to believe seriously, remembering how the crooked arrows describe a curve and deviate from the target, that the blissful gunpowder was crooked. He promised, then, not to close his eyes or turn his head at the time of shooting to see from which side the shot was tilted; but an unexpected setback deprived him of this experience. Cañuela, who had just put a thick handful of pebbles into the canyon, suddenly exclaimed from the trunk on which he was perched, all in alarm:

–The shotgun has no space left!

Petaca looked at the rifle in his hands and then at his cousin full of surprise, without understanding what those words meant. The blonde then pointed to the mouth of the cannon, through which part of the last cue was sticking out. He inclined the gun and felt the opening with his fingers and was convinced that there was no way to put there another grain of gunpowder or anything else. His forehead frowned. He was beginning to guess why the gun had gained so much weight. He turned to the ranch, which they had been approaching as the afternoon progressed, and reflected on the probable consequences of that event, deciding, after a while, to retreat and leave Cañuela the glory of getting out of the quagmire. He knew too well the grandfather's temperament to be within his reach. But his fertile imagination devised another plan that seemed so magnificent to him that, discarding the projected flight, he planted himself in front of his cousin, who, very restless, had observed him up to that point without daring to open his mouth, and spoke to him with animation of something that must have been very unusual, because Cañuela, with tears in his eyes, was reluctant to second him. But he ended up submitting as always, and both them gathered dry leaves and branches eagerly, piling them on the ground. When they believed there was enough, Cañuela took out of his unfathomable pockets a box of matches and set fire to the pyre. As soon as the flames rose a little, Petaca took the rifle and laid it on the fire, retiring at once, the two of them, to contemplate at a distance the progress of the fire. A few minutes passed and Petaca was going to come closer again to add more fuel, when a formidable boom deafened them. The bonfire was scattered to the four winds, and sinister whistles furrowed the air.

Petaca was as pale as his cousin, but his energetic nature made him recover very soon, heading for the site of the explosion, which was as clean as if it had been raked. No matter how much he looked, he found no trace of the rifle.

Cañuela, who had followed him crying his heart out, suddenly stopped, petrified by terror. At the top of the hill, thirty paces away, the grandfather's high silhouette stood out, advancing with great strides. He seemed to be possessed of terrible anger. He gesticulated in loud voices, his right hand held high, wielding a smoking firebrand that bore an extraordinary resemblance to a shotgun casing. Petaca, who had seen the apparition, at the same time as his cousin, ran down the slope of the hill, hitting his thighs with the palms of his hands, while whistling his favorite air. While he was running, he examined the casing of the weapon, he could very well find, in turn, the barrel or even a small piece with which a blunderbuss would be made to shot and kill plumbeous rails in the lagoon.

www.ingramcontent.com/pod-product-compliance
Lightning Source LLC
Chambersburg PA
CBHW071440260626
47170CB00008B/2784